THE JILTED BRIDE'S
BILLIONAIRE HUSBAND

A CAPROCK CANYON ROMANCE BOOK FIVE

BREE LIVINGSTON

Edited by
CHRISTINA SCHRUNK

Merry Christmas, everyone.
May it be a time of joy, laughter, and love with those you call family and friends.

CHAPTER 1

P acing his room, Bandit Ochoa lifted his phone to his ear. Maybe, just maybe, his best friend could give him advice. If not Bear, maybe the combined powers of him and his wife, Winnie, would come to his rescue.

The line picked up, and the familiar voice filtered through the phone. "Hey, Bandit. How are you?"

Just the sound of Bear's voice gave Bandit a little relief. Although he'd seen the Wests just a few weeks ago at his grandpa's funeral, he'd been away from home for over a year now, and the itch to return was worse than ever, especially considering what he'd learned an hour ago.

"W-w-well, I've b-b-been better."

Next thing Bandit knew, the video feature of his phone was ringing, and he tapped the screen. Bear's face, framed by pictures of family and new additions, came into view. "Now, tell me what's going on."

Bandit walked to a nearby chair in his grandpa's study and sat. "Th-th-the reading of th-th-the will was t-t-today."

Nodding, Bear's lips pressed into a hard line. "Is it bad?"

"W-w-worse than bad."

His friend sat forward a little, bringing his face closer. "Did he owe money or something? Because I—"

That was Bear. If his family was in trouble, he was willing to drop everything and anything to help. Bandit was just blessed enough to be considered a member of the fold.

Bandit held his hand up to cut Bear off. "N-n-no, Bear. I've g-g-got all the money I need." Well, he would if he could figure out how to grant his grandfather's wishes.

"Then what? If he didn't owe money..." The sentence trailed off. Bear's mind was working over-time, trying to come up with something.

Except Bandit knew there was no way to ever come up with what his grandpa had plagued him with. "I-I-I have to g-g-get married."

Bear looked just as stunned as Bandit felt. Who in their right mind would make a fella get married to inherit money? It wasn't just money he needed to consider, either. Charities would go without, people would lose jobs, and a host of other things. His grandpa, Mauricio Ochoa, had left no stone unturned when it came to forcing Bandit's hand, and as his only living heir, the entire operation fell to Bandit. It was the middle of September, and he had sixty days from October 1st to find someone to call Mrs. Ochoa.

"You don't need the money, Bandit. You have a home here. Shoot, you know that. Kin doesn't let kin go without." Bear squared his shoulders. "He's got no right to force that on you."

A small smile lifted Bandit's lips. Bear had once been the focus of his sister's insistence on dating, so he knew all too well what it was like to feel pressured. Only, Winnie came from that, and Bear loved her more than life itself.

"Y-y-you don't understand. He t-t-tied my hands. If I-I-I don't, the money will j-j-just sit in an account." Bandit paused. "He's got ch-ch-charities and busi-nesses. N-n-not just here in the S-S-States, but all over the w-w-world. If I don't get m-m-married, it all stops. A-a-all of it. I either g-g-get married or destroy p-p-people's lives and l-l-livelihoods."

3

Once he was married, the money would flow like nothing had changed, and Bandit would receive a generous allowance for the first year of marriage. After that first year of marriage, the full estate would be signed over to him, making him wealthier than he could have ever imagined.

Bear sucked in a sharp breath and let it out in a whistle. "Why on earth would he do that?"

Well, that was the billion-dollar question right there. The word sadistic came to mind, but Bandit knew better. His grandpa was one of the kindest, gentlest souls to walk the earth. "I-I-I don't know yet. Th-th-the lawyer gave me-me-me a flash drive. Said all the a-a-answers were on that—a-a-according to what my grandfather t-t-told him."

Bear rubbed his knuckles along his jaw, seemingly just as speechless as Bandit.

A moment later, Winnie came into view and smiled. "Hey, Bandit." Her head tilted. "Are you okay? Do we need to hunt someone down?"

We. The word tugged at his gut. Bandit wanted to be part of a we. But...the way he stuttered. Who would want him? How many times had he told his grandpa that? A sigh of frustration poured from Bandit's core. The same man he loved and respected had put him in a horrible predicament. Why? Just why would he do that?

"Bandit?" Winnie's voice broke through his thoughts.

Without realizing it, he'd gone silent and his gaze had drifted to the floor. He lifted his head. "I-I-I have to get married." According to his grandpa, he wasn't getting any younger and thirty-eight was old enough to have the sense to find someone.

Her jaw slowly dropped. "Have to?"

Bear quickly brought her in on the conversation, telling her the entire thing. When he was finished, she shook her head. "Well, it sounds like you don't have a choice."

"What?" Bear blurted. "He certainly does have a choice. Forcing a man to get married ain't right."

Winnie looked pointedly at Bandit, and her eyes narrowed. "Give me one moment with my husband."

Bandit nodded.

The screen went black, and the silence stretched out. Minute after minute ticked by until Bandit thought they'd gone into battle and neither had come out alive. Just when he was about to end the call, Bear and Winnie came back into view, and the sound was back on.

"Bandit, I have an idea, but you need to let me talk to someone, okay?" Winnie asked.

"T-t-talk to who?" Bandit asked.

Winnie shook her head. "No, not until I talk to them. There's no point in mentioning names until I know."

Bear shrugged. "You could do what I did." He pulled Winnie onto his lap as he sat down. "You could post on that matchmaker website. Find a fake wife. Maybe you'll be as blessed as I am." He kissed the tip of her nose.

Hardly. It was much easier to find someone when you didn't sound like an idiot. There was no point in saying anything, though. The Wests were nothing if not loyal, and anyone who couldn't see Bandit's heart didn't deserve him.

What they didn't consider was the other person. What if they deserved better than him? That's what his dad had said right before he left. That he didn't want to be stuck with someone who sounded stupid. Bandit's mom had always tried to soothe those words, but they'd dug their claws in deep. Alcohol, drugs...it didn't matter why his dad had said them, just that they were said.

Shaking his head, Bandit replied, "I don't know

wh-wh-what to do. I don't w-w-want anyone suffering because of me, but marriage isn't something to-to-to trifle with."

Winnie leaned in. "We'll figure out something." She smiled. "Bandit, you're a good man. A woman—any woman—should be lucky to have you."

He waved her off. "Aw...d-d-don't you start."

Her eyes narrowed. "You stop, or when you get here for Christmas, I'll whoop ya."

A burst of laughter poured out of Bandit with Bear joining in. The scary part was that Bandit could see her doing it. "I-I-I need to go. I'm g-g-going to see what my g-g-grandpa has to s-s-say for himself. See if he makes a-a-any sense at all."

They said their goodbyes, and Bandit ended the call. He did find himself curious as to who Winnie was talking about. He shook his head, trying to clear the thoughts. Even if she did have someone in mind, the moment they heard him speak, it would be over and he'd be back to square one. Bear's idea wasn't any better. Did he honestly want to get married knowing it would end? That wasn't what his momma had taught him before she died.

Marriage was sacred. You entered it knowing that the other person would fail you at some point—and that you'd fail them—but you'd always work through it. It wasn't fifty-fifty. It was everything you've got from both people involved. It meant love and honor and devotion, even in times of turmoil and pain. How she could believe those things after how Bandit's dad had left them was still a mystery to him.

He stuck the flash drive into the slot on the desktop and waited for the prompts to display, clicking okay to play once it popped up on the screen. "Okay, Grandpa, you've got some explaining to do."

About the only time Bandit didn't stutter was when he was completely alone. For the life of him, he didn't know why, but the pressure would build in his chest, his head would swim, and his tongue didn't work when he was around people. It didn't matter how close they were, and Bandit had no explanation as to why it worked like that. Neither did any of the speech thera-pists his mom had taken him to as a child.

The film flickered to life, and Bandit's grandpa appeared on the screen, smiling like there wasn't a thing wrong—even though Parkinson's had him shaky all over. "Oh, boy, I bet you are as mad as hornet right about now."

Bandit grunted a laugh. Not mad. Confused. Blind-sided. Maybe the anger would come later.

"You're probably wondering why I did what I did,

making you get married, but there is no one person on this earth that I love more than you. Well, your grandma, of course, but I'm talking about the living."

"Yeah, I know." Bandit knew it was ridiculous to respond, but in a way, it felt like he could have one more conversation with the man.

His grandpa shook his head, smiling. "Boy, you are everything your daddy never could be. Intelligent, kind-hearted, loyal." His grandpa looked down. "I was partly—wholly—to blame for that. I should've been home more. I should've been more open and honest, but I guess you can see things a little more clearly when you're ninety-six."

The only thing Bandit could note was that never had his grandpa looked his age until just that moment. "Aw, you did what you could. You tried to make it right."

From what Bandit learned from his grandpa's small staff, he'd tried to mend the relationship with Bandit's dad, only to be rebuffed time after time. It went on for years with Bandit's dad begging for money and promising to change, only to dive deeper into drugs and alcohol. Eventually, Bandit's grandpa realized there was no changing someone who didn't want to be changed.

A deathbed confession from Bandit's dad was the

only mention that he'd had a son. One he'd left in Texas without so much as a care or thought. The second his grandpa found out, he'd sent people looking for Bandit.

Life had changed the day Bandit met his grandpa. He'd gone from having a surrogate family to having a grandpa he'd learned to love. He was the kind of man Bandit wished his dad would have been. It still puzzled him how a man like his dad could come from a man like his grandpa.

His grandpa continued, "You know all about that, though, so I won't rehash it. I suspect you're more interested in the conditions of your inheritance."

"Ya don't say." Bandit chuckled and shook his head.

"Now, I know you and I don't see eye to eye on finding a woman, but, Bandit, you're a good man. I don't think I could be prouder of the man you've become." His grandpa paused, looking straight into the camera. "My boy, you deserve someone to love. You've got far too much to offer to hide away, thinking you aren't worthy to be loved."

Pulling his gaze from the screen, Bandit's shoulders sagged. "I'm not."

"I know you probably don't think too highly of me right now, but, son, I'm doing this for you. There's a woman out there who's looking for you, and you're looking for her. I didn't do what I should have for your daddy, but I sure am going to do everything I can for you. Even pushing you to do something you might not want to do. Perhaps..." His grandpa's voice cracked, and Bandit jerked his gaze to the screen.

Often, the man would choke up talking about Bandit's dad. The grief for that relationship weighed heavily on the man, and based on that, Bandit couldn't fault him, even if Bandit did disagree with the method.

"You gave me something I thought I'd never have. You showed me that your daddy had good in him. No way in this world would you be here if he didn't. I failed him, but I won't fail you." A smile lifted the man's lips. "Now, go find a woman."

His grandpa looked at someone standing behind the camera and said, "I'm good." And then, like another thought had hit him, he looked back into the camera. "Now, you're a smart man, and before you get the wild idea that you can get married and not live with this woman—that's not how it works. You'll live together the full year or it doesn't count." He winked. "I'm old, but my mind ain't."

The video went black, and Bandit stared at the screen.

Go find a woman.

"Go find a unicorn." Likely easier than what his

grandpa was asking. Lord, have mercy on him. He lifted his gaze to the ceiling, willing whoever was out there to hear his plea, dread pooling in his stomach that in sixty days, one way or another, his life would change forever.

CHAPTER 2

Pulling her door open, Skye Alvarez yawned as she said, "No, Mrs. Dahal, I swear I don't have a pet raccoon." She blinked as the midafternoon sun hit her square in the face. That's what she got for hiding in her home for so long.

"Uh..." Her friend, Winnie West, tilted her head, a smile forming on her lips. "What?"

Skye rubbed the sleep from her eyes and raked her hand through her hair with a sigh. "Winnie?"

"Uh-huh. Whatcha doing?" Her friend's cheery voice did nothing to help clear the fog.

"What time is it?" Another yawn poured from Skye.

"Two in the afternoon," Winnie replied. "But, um... what's this about a pet raccoon?"

With a wave, Skye stepped back so Winnie could

enter her small rented townhome in Amarillo. With all the bills from her wedding, it was all she could afford. "Come on in."

Winnie shuffled inside as Skye explained the weird greeting. "I've got a neighbor who's convinced I have a pet raccoon because she finds one in the dumpster every morning."

"Well, you do get points for the most original greeting I've ever heard." Winnie chuckled.

IF IT WERE anyone other than Winnie, Skye would be running around her place trying to pick up the dirty dishes, shoving the mountain of laundry on her couch into a closet, and turning on the wax warmer. They'd only known each other roughly a year, and during that time, they'd become the best of friends.

"Sorry for the mess," Skye said, pushing the mass of laundry on the couch aside so Winnie could sit.

Winne dropped into the seat. "Are you doing okay?"

Okay. If Skye said yes, it would be a lie, and Winnie would know it based solely on the state of her home. Pulling her robe closed as she sat in the recliner she parked herself in day after day, she said, "Not really."

"I know it has to be hard." Winnie would know

since she was maid of honor at Skye's…her heart hurt at the thought of the word.

It was September, and by now, Skye and her now ex-husband, Robert Faulks, would be going on seven and half months of marriage. As far as she knew, they'd had a perfect marriage. He had a great job at a CPA firm, and she owned her own business. They loved each other—so she thought.

Instead, she was paying caterers for food, flowers, the venue, and the DJ…for a marriage that lasted just over three months. If she'd known then, she would've had a simpler wedding. Instead, she'd spent too much money on something she thought would last forever.

Tears threatened to pour yet again. "I just wish I'd known…" If it were only the bills, it would be hard but possible. Those added to the other thing she'd received…

"Skye, you can't keep living like this. It's been four and a half months since he left. Are you going to let that jerk live in your head and ruin your life? I know it was terrible what he did. I'm not saying it wasn't."

"You don't understand." Skye groaned.

"Then explain it to me. I've offered to help with the bills. You know how Bear feels about him."

A snort popped out of Skye. Her friend had married a billionaire, and Bear West was one of the sweetest men on earth. As soon as he found out what happened, he'd offered to help, but Skye just didn't feel right about that. The bills were just money. They weren't what was wrecking her heart.

Winnie slipped off the couch and kneeled in front of Skye, pushing back her hair. "Tell me what's going on. I love you, Skye."

Lifting tear-filled eyes to Winnie, Skye held her gaze. "I'm pregnant."

"I kinda suspected," replied Winnie, smiling.

"You did?" Along with surprise, a tiny sliver of relief flowed through Skye.

"Does Robert know?"

"Yeah, I told him as soon as I found out. He was a little upset but said we'd talk more when he returned from his business trip." Skye sniffed, reliving the memory. He'd been on plenty of trips while they were dating and engaged. "Then, wham. Divorce papers."

"Oh, sweetheart." Winnie inhaled through her nose and huffed. "Well, he's not worth the dirt he walks on, then. You and the baby are better off without him."

Placing her hand on her five-and-a-half-month-pregnant stomach, Skye let the word "baby" roll through her mind. It's not that she didn't want the baby; she just knew being a single mom wouldn't be easy.

Plus, how was she going to tell her parents? They'd most likely say that at twenty-eight, she should've been wiser about picking her husband, and she couldn't disagree. They'd be upset with Robert, but her mom wouldn't hesitate to place blame on Skye as well. After all, she was the one who married him. So far, she'd managed to keep them in the dark by wearing baggy shirts when they visited. Her lips trembled as she pictured the scene with her and her parents.

"Stop that right there!" Winnie practically growled. "A baby is a gift. Maybe not an expected gift sometimes, but a gift nonetheless." Her friend patted her hand. "It's not your fault he left. I know you've said your parents can be hard on you, but they'll understand that."

Skye had met Winnie when she got engaged to Bear. They'd chosen Skye's shop, A Floral Skye, in Amarillo as their florist. Skye had liked them immediately. Down to earth, sweet, and friendly. From there, their friendship had blossomed—so to speak. Her cousin Ashley Alvarez was managing the shop currently, which was a blessing too. If not for her, Skye couldn't imagine the mess she'd be in.

If only Skye's mom were as forgiving as Winnie. They'd always been at odds with each other. Everything from what Skye wore to her lack of makeup and her weight. She could only imagine how disappointed her mom would be once she found out Skye was pregnant. Divorce was bad enough. Add a baby to the mix, and her mom would maybe not disown Skye, but it would come close.

Taking both of Skye's hands, Winnie squeezed them. "Okay, the pouting and pining and all that is over. I've got a plan."

Skye's eyebrows knitted together. "Easier said than done."

"Well, yeah," Winnie replied, looking around the room. "You're living in a cave. You need some sunshine, good food, and...I have a favor I need to ask."

"What kind of favor?" Skye quirked an eyebrow up.

"The kind that needs some buttering up before I ask." Winnie shot her a wide, cheesy grin.

Buttering up? "What could you possibly be asking me?"

Her friend shook her head. "Nope. I need a near food coma for this one."

Skye's jaw dropped, and then her eyes narrowed. "I'm not putting a fork to my mouth without some explanation."

"Oh yeah? How about filet mignon with a mushroom-and-red-wine-infused demi-glace, with baby carrots slow cooked in organic honey along with bacon-wrapped asparagus? And for dessert? Crème brûlée pecan pie with chocolate drizzle."

Using the back of her hand, Skye wiped her mouth, expecting to pull it away with saliva covering it. Winnie's cooking. The woman could throw down a mean meal. Plus, Gabby's pie? She could pull secrets from the CIA with that sort of confection. Totally worth the two-hour drive too. "You're evil."

"It's a big favor."

"I guess I could at least hear you out." She gave a weak smile.

"Absolutely. You are free to say no, but..." Her friend seemed to decide against the rest of the sentence and shook her head.

Skye narrowed her eyes. "When is this food coma of a meal going to be cooked?"

"Have you got any plans tonight?"

A grunted laugh came from the back of Skye's throat. "No."

Winnie stood. "Okay, then get yourself together, and I'll see you at the restaurant tonight at eight thirty."

Skye tilted her head. "It's Sunday. You close at seven on Sundays."

"This is a special dinner. Just dress like you

normally would, and I'll see ya at the restaurant." Winnie walked to the door. "I'll see you tonight." She opened the door and paused. "And keep an open mind. We're not just talking about you anymore. We've got a baby to think of too."

Just like Winnie West. If there was a problem, it wasn't faced alone. "I know. I'll see you tonight."

SKYE TAPPED on the door of Winnie's restaurant and then ran her hand down the front of her maxi dress. She'd paired it with a light sweater and flats to round out the casual feel of the outfit. If nothing else, she was comfortable and her belly wouldn't be in the spotlight. It was just a pooch at the moment—well…a bigger one since she wasn't exactly skinny to start with, but comfort was something high on her want-list as of late.

The door opened, and Winnie greeted her with a smile as she waved her inside. "You look so good."

"I think I killed an entire pack of razors trying to get my legs shaved. With my luck, I'll need a plumber to fish out the Tribble I put down the drain." She held in a laugh as she realized she'd watched entirely too much *Star Trek* while she'd been hiding from the world.

Winnie cackled. "Oh my goodness. You are a mess."

Skye shrugged. "It's the truth." Her gaze raked across the restaurant and landed on a table that looked like it was set for two. "Is it just us?"

"No, but first, I need your promise to keep an open mind—"

"NO! I am not interested—" She tried to move to the door, and Winnie caught her.

She clapped a hand over Skye's mouth. "Listen for a second. Will you listen?"

Slowly, Skye nodded, and Winnie withdrew her hand. "I'll lick you the next time you do that," Skye said.

"Then don't make me do it." Her friend huffed and ushered Skye to the table, pulling out a chair for her. "Now, an open mind and don't talk until I'm done."

"Fine." Skye lowered herself into the seat. "I'll listen, but I get some of that crème brûlée to take home."

"Whatever," Winnie said, taking her seat across from Skye. She took a deep breath. "Okay, I have a good friend. Bear's best friend, Bandit Ochoa."

Skye had a vague recollection of meeting the man.

He'd been wonderful to Winnie. "Is this the same man who let you use this restaurant space?"

"Yep, same sweet fella." Winnie grinned. "His grandfather found him a little over a year ago now, and he was taking care of the man until he passed away a few weeks ago."

Skye's shoulders sagged. "That's awful." In the back of her mind niggled, *And that has what to do with me?*

"It hit him pretty hard. His grandpa was a generous man. From what Bandit's said, his grandpa has several charities here in the States, as well as abroad, plus several businesses that employ thousands of people." Winnie waved her hand around the restaurant. "I mean, if it weren't for Bandit, I wouldn't have this place."

Skye blew out a big puff of air. "Sounds like the old man was loaded. Also sounds like he tried to give back too." Nice guy. Still didn't answer the question buzzing in her brain.

"He was loaded. Like…billionaire loaded."

Good thing Skye wasn't drinking. Winnie would be wearing it. "Billionaire?" Then the word *duh* pranced through her mind. He couldn't have all those charities and businesses if he didn't have that kind of money.

"Yeah, and this is the part where you come in."

Winnie hesitated. "The part where you need to have an open mind."

Skye braced herself and nodded. She could already tell she wasn't going to like it.

"His grandfather left a condition that Bandit has to fulfill before he can inherit the money. And it's a big condition."

"Okay."

Winnie chewed her lip. "Now, if you knew Bandit, you'd know he wouldn't do it if it weren't for the consequences of not doing it."

"Oooookay." If Winnie didn't get to the point soon, Skye was going to poke her with a fork.

"If he doesn't do this thing, then the money stops going to all those charities and businesses. It'll sit in the account and just do nothing."

"And this thing Bandit has to do is…?" She let the sentence trail off so Winnie could answer.

"He has to get married and stay married for a year."

Skye opened her mouth to speak, but words failed her. Poor guy. "And that has what…to…do…" Her eyes widened as she realized why she'd been lured to the middle of nowhere with the promise of food. She poked her chest with her index finger, blinking. "You want me to *marry* him?" The last word hit an octave high enough to make Mariah Carry jealous.

Winnie chewed her lip and nodded, her eyebrows knitting together. "Skye, he's sweet and kind and loving and wonderful. I also know you don't want to get married again so quickly, but you have bills from the wedding and..." Winnie pointed to Skye's tummy. "And a baby to consider. We could make this mutually beneficial."

"So he's wanting to purchase a wife for a year?" she asked, still trying to wrap her mind around the situation.

"Uh, well..." She grimaced. "He may not know about that part yet."

Skye sucked in a sharp breath, palming her forehead. "Oh, Winnie. What are you doing?"

"I love him, and I love you. And both of you need something the other has. He needs a wife, and you need a college fund for the baby. Plus, you'd get to spend Christmas with me." Her worried look morphed into a smile like this whole thing didn't sound bizarre. Which, given how she'd met Bear, wasn't all that farfetched of an idea. "He'll be living in Caprock Canyon, which means you'd get to eat my cooking, Gabby's pies, and Bandit's famous cinnamon rolls."

Even with the promise of those hip-busters, Skye still felt like she was in the middle of a prank gone wrong. "This is a lot to take in. Marriage isn't something you just do. I just…"

"I know, and I know it's a lot to think about. That's kind of why I invited you here. That way you could meet him and make an informed decision."

Skye's eyes widened. "Tonight? Have you lost your mind?" She looked down at herself. "I look like a bohemian hobo. If you had told me—"

"You look beautiful, and if I told you, you would never have come."

She opened her mouth to disagree and clamped it shut. Nope, she would have put the kibosh on it the very second Winnie uttered it. "Winnie, I'm just barely divorced. I'm pregnant. The last thing I need is a man making things even messier. He's not going to want to take care of another man's child."

"Just meet him. That's all I ask. Just give him a chance. Please." Winnie leveled the most pitiful, sad face Skye had ever witnessed. "Please. If you meet him and decide against it, I will drive to Amarillo every weekend for six months and cook you whatever you want."

Skye's eyebrows went to her hairline. "For real?" One eyebrow remained lifted. "And all I have to is meet him?"

"Yes, and, *no*, you can't say hello to him and leave."

She gave Skye a menacing look. "Have dinner with him. Talk to him. Then actually think about it."

"Fine, but only because you're going to be putting miles on that sweet little F-150 you've got. And, you better be prepared to cook up a storm 'cause Mama is eating for two."

Winnie stuck her hand out. "Deal."

Skye held in a gasp. Winnie was entirely too eager to make this wager. "You think I'm gonna change my mind, don't you?"

"Yep." She popped the *p* at the end of the word.

"You're a..." Skye didn't finish the sentence as a knock came from the front door.

Winnie jumped to her feet. "Wonderful person, and now I have to answer the door." She flashed a wide smile and nearly danced to the door.

Groaning, Skye slouched forward. What she should be doing is marching right out of there after giving Winnie a chewing out. Instead, her gut said she needed to think this through. Whether that was from hunger or the promise of a college fund, she wasn't sure. Maybe a lot of both?

Fine. She'd meet the man, have a fantastic meal, and wish Bandit Ochoa the best of luck in finding a woman to marry as she happily carted herself and the sack of crème brûlée home, with six months of Winnie's cooking ahead of her.

Satisfied with her level-headed response, she pulled her shoulders back and smiled. This was going to be a breeze.

CHAPTER 3

Bandit pulled his Stetson from his head and held it at his side. He had no idea what Winnie had planned, but knowing her, it could be anything. The only thing he wished was that he'd had more notice before driving to Caprock Canyon. Between the loss of sleep over his grandpa's condition and passing away and the long trip, he was plum near exhausted.

"Hey, Bandit," Winnie said, sliding out the door and shutting it behind her. "You okay?" She hugged him and rubbed his back. "I've missed you so much."

He returned the hug, his cheeks warming. "Aw, I-I-I've missed you too."

She leaned back, keeping her hands clasped on his biceps. "I need you to hear me out."

Warning bells blared. *What* was this woman up to? "Wh-wh-what?"

"That marriage clause of your grandpa's. I think I have a solution."

His eyes narrowed. "Oookay."

She took a deep breath, looked over her shoulder, and turned back to him. "My friend Skye Alvarez is inside. She's the sweetest woman you'll ever meet, but she's...she's had it rough."

He nodded, allowing her to continue without interruption. There was nothing nice to say about a man like that.

"Earlier this year, her husband of three months went on a business trip, and a week later, she was being served divorce papers. Didn't talk to her or tell her what was wrong. Nothing. Just took off. It broke her heart." Winnie cleared her throat. "I don't know how you'll feel about this next part, but just continue to keep that mind of yours open."

His interest was certainly piqued. What—

"She's pregnant. I sort of suspected it when she turned into a hermit and wouldn't leave her house in the last few months. She confirmed it earlier today."

"P-p-pregnant?" he squeaked out. It would have come out that way whether he stuttered or not.

"Now, don't freak out." She chuckled. "But, yes,

she's about five and a half months along. She has a ton of bills from the wedding that her jerk ex-husband left her with, and now she has a baby coming who she'll need to care for."

Peering around her, Bandit hoped he could catch a glimpse of the woman Winnie was talking about. He couldn't imagine promising to love and honor someone and then running off, but he sure knew what abandonment felt like. He suspected they were much the same. "That's a-a-awful."

Winnie dropped her hands to her sides. "It is. Now, you need to marry someone, and she's got bills and a baby. She's not ready to be in a relationship just yet, and you've got a time problem. I think the two of you could hammer out an agreement that would benefit you both."

Buy a wife? His mind reeled.

The second he started shaking his head, Winnie's eyes got a fierce look in them. She crossed her arms over her chest. "Don't you shake your head at me, Bandit Ochoa. This is a good idea. I know it is. Just go meet her. If you hate each other, no harm, no foul. But if you hit it off enough to put up with each other for a year, then it's two problems solved with one stone."

Bandit ran his hand through his hair. Winnie was never the poster child for taking *no* for an answer, but she *did* have to deal with Bear. It was probably just second nature at this point, given how stubborn her husband was.

"Just have dinner with her. My treat. All you've lost is a couple of hours." Winnie sandwiched his hand between hers. "Try. That's all I'm asking."

They held each other's gaze a moment until Bandit cracked. "All r-r-right. I'll m-m-meet her."

A smile stretched on Winnie's lips, and her face lit up. "Thank you." Using her hand, she pushed the door open and held it for him to pass through. "Come on. Let me introduce you."

Bandit followed Winnie to the table, and his pulse jumped as Skye came into view. Winnie was a beautiful woman, but this woman she was introducing him to? She was a raven-haired angel with honey-colored skin. He couldn't talk well to start with, but there was a good chance she'd render him mute.

Skye gave him a tiny grin. "Hi."

Bandit just stared. Her dark silky tresses cascaded over her shoulders, slick and straight. Equally dark eyes locked with his gaze, and all he could do was wonder what treasures they might hold. He didn't particularly hold a belief in love at first sight, but there was a whole lot of like happening.

Winnie cleared her throat and said, "Skye Alvarez,

this is Christopher "Bandit" Ochoa. Bandit, this is Skye."

Skye's skin peeked out from the loose light-blue sweater she wore, and the dress with splashes of color on a white backdrop accentuated her heart-shaped face and full, dark-pink lips. All of which accentuated her curves, an attribute he'd always found attractive on women. Add the glow of pregnancy, and she was one hot mama.

An elbow from Winnie jerked him out of his stupor. "H-h-hi." He winced. His heart thundered in his chest to the point that he couldn't hear himself think. What must this beautiful woman think of a guy like him? "It's n-n-nice to meet y-y-you."

Winnie looked from Skye to Bandit and grinned wide. "Okay, I'll finish up your dinner and get it plated while you two get acquainted."

As she left, Bandit took a seat across from Skye, setting his hat on the edge of the table. "Th-th-this is…"

"A situation with a list of adverbs longer than I can wrangle into a sentence."

He laughed and nodded. "Y-y-yes. I'm s-s-sorry I…"

She shrugged. "For stuttering? Nothing to be sorry for. I'm pretty nervous myself." A soft sigh whooshed out of her. "The elephant in the room is that I'm pregnant. The fact that you didn't run the second Winnie told you gives you at least a few positive points to start with." She grinned.

"S-s-she told me. Rotten sc-sc-scoundrel."

"And you get two more points." Her smile brightened, making her already pretty face even more so. She cast her gaze to the table as her shoulders rounded. "I was stupid. I—"

Something about her spoke to him just then. He covered her hand with his. "N-n-no, you trrrrusted h-h-him. Th-th-that's not stupid." Warmth spread from her skin and soaked into his. "A m-m-man that r-r-runs from his ch-ch-child is path-th-thetic." So much for those relaxation exercises to help him not stutter as much. They were useless in the presence of Skye.

Tear-rimmed eyes lifted to his. "Please don't feel sorry for me."

Shaking his head, he said, "No." It took all his energy just to make a simple response.

"Okay, you two. I've got the best meal I've ever prepared on these two plates." Winnie announced her presence with a swoosh of the door and strode to the table, setting a plate in front of each of them. She looked from Bandit to Skye and back, trying to hide a smile as her gaze flicked from his face to his hand on

Skye's. "I'll be in the back if you need anything." She returned to the kitchen.

Bandit needed a new tongue so he could actually get his thoughts out. Things like, *What kind of man walks out on his wife and his child?* Bandit doubted she'd want anything to do with him once the evening was over, but when he did find a woman who took sympathy on him, he'd make sure Skye and her baby were taken care of—of course, he'd tell his…wife, but he'd make it happen one way or another.

Maybe Skye could or should have made better decisions, but Bandit wasn't without a few poor choices in his life. He wouldn't be throwing rocks. He'd be lending support if she wanted it. Deep down, he hoped she did.

ALL THE BUTTERFLIES coalescing in Skye's stomach made her jittery. If she could, she'd douse them in bug killer. She did not need to be attracted to Bandit. Not with a baby on the way. Plus, her judgment was completely suspect at this point based on her last pick for a husband.

Still, a zing of electricity had ripped through her veins the second he put his hand over hers. The gesture was sweet too. Sure didn't hurt that he was hotter than Texas asphalt in August. He was tall and dark-haired with broad shoulders she could see herself leaning her head against.

Dressed in jeans and a checked button-up, he looked every bit the working man she'd always found attractive. His hands weren't as calloused as she liked, but he'd spent the last year taking care of his grandpa. That was a good reason for soft hands.

He was frustrated, though. She could see in his eyes that his speech bothered him. It would be a lie if she said it wouldn't take getting used to, but so was the idea of her being pregnant. Then again, billions hung in the balance. Maybe he was just that desperate.

"This looks pretty delicious." Man, it'd been a while since she'd had Winnie's cooking. Her mouth watered as she cut off a piece of steak and took a bite. She moaned a little too loudly, but she didn't care. "Oh, it's so juicy and tender."

After saying a quick blessing, which she found endearing, he followed her by slicing off a piece and eating it. "Y-y-you aren't k-k-kidding."

Robert's habit of just digging in had rubbed off on her. She'd grown up saying a blessing before eating. Now, she felt a little bad for not waiting. Another point in Bandit's favor. Skye looked at Bandit as she cut another piece of steak off. "I've been told you have famous cinnamon rolls."

He lowered his head, but she saw the blush creep into his cheeks and run to the tips of his ears. Probably one of his most endearing qualities so far. Unlike Robert, who thought the sun rose and set with him. Arrogant jerk.

"It's j-j-just a recipe m-m-my mom used." He shrugged and forked a few carrots into his mouth. "Man, these carrots."

She abandoned her steak and stabbed a few with her fork. "I love her carrots in honey." The flavor exploded on her tongue the second they hit it. "Ohhhh. That was worth the drive."

Nodding, Bandit finished off the carrots and went straight to the asparagus. He cut a few and paused, keeping his head down. His shoulders seemed to sag. "I've missed being home, but I couldn't leave my grandpa. Other than my momma, he's the only blood family who ever loved me."

The first thing that struck Skye was that he didn't stutter. Apparently, it was just nerves causing that little problem. The second and sweetest thing was that he'd been homesick and still stayed to take care of his family. That took sacrifice. When had Robert ever sacrificed anything? And why was it that she was only now seeing that?

"That was kind of you to stay with him."

He jerked his head up, his eyes wide. "I-I-I…"

"You get nervous."

"Y-y-yeah." His eyebrows knitted together. "Y-y-you'd think I'd b-b-be fine since I-I-I've known the W-W-Wests for so long."

Boy, did she sympathize. Robert hadn't helped with her confidence either. Aside from her own issues with her weight, he'd only added to them by reminding her about it any chance he got. Plus, he was self-centered, and if things didn't benefit him, he didn't care. When had she started overlooking his flaws? Better, if she was that bad at judging character, did she need to be hitching her horse to someone new?

"Not really. I have a florist shop, and every time I make a flower arrangement, I fret over it. What if they don't like it? I've loved flowers since I was itty-bitty, and I know I'm good at what I do. Everyone has their self-doubts."

"Could I ask y-y-you a question?" He caught her gaze and held it. "Y-y-you don't h-h-have to answer."

Anytime something ended with that sort of sentence, it was usually something the person being asked didn't want to talk about. Did she want to answer questions she might not like?

"Sure." Her heart spoke for her before her head got in a word edgewise.

This time he wouldn't quite meet her eyes. "M-m-my grandpa—well, my m-m-momma too—t-t-taught me th-th-that if you h-h-have the means and s-s-someone's in n-n-need, you h-h-help them."

Skye remained quiet despite the prideful side of her screaming that she didn't need help.

"I-I-I know Winnie told you my circumstances, but I'll help you in any way I can." He lowered his gaze, pushing his food around on his plate. "Y-y-you don't have to h-h-help me."

Either he was absolutely the kindest man she'd ever met or he was yanking her chain. Her inclination leaned toward compassionate. "Why?"

Lifting his head, he said, "B-b-because my d-d-dad left m-m-me, and I know wh-wh-what it's like. No one should be d-d-done like you were." His gaze dipped to her tummy. "And y-y-you have a little one coming. You don't n-n-need to be w-w-worried." He clamped his mouth shut and squeezed his eyes closed, huffing. "You sh-sh-shouldn't have to-to worry about anything but cravings and enjoying your p-p-pregnancy."

Her wacky hormones were making her the weepiest woman to ever live. Tears threatened to spill, and it was all she could do to hold them back. In a perfect world, that's exactly what she would have wanted. "Thank you. For the offer. I appreciate it."

Skye stared at him. She should have known Winnie wouldn't have set up this meeting slash impromptu date if she had any doubts Skye would say no. That wretched little redhead.

Even as she fumed, the question of whether she'd marry him or not became clearer and clearer. He needed to claim his inheritance, and...she wanted more than money. She wanted a hand to hold while she went through her pregnancy. If nothing else, he was a nice man, and living in Caprock Canyon would be fun.

Instead of the outright *no* she'd planned, there was a *maybe* stamped on the whole thing. For the moment, she'd at least think about it.

CHAPTER 4

A month and a half later, Skye looked up at the courthouse in front of her, wondering how her life choices led her to that exact spot. Well, not her pregnancy. She knew very well what her choice had been that night. Stupid.

Rubbing a hand over her seven-month tummy, she took a deep breath and smiled. Not stupid, just unwise. Once she'd decided to keep the baby, she'd promised herself to look at the situation like an unexpected gift. Harboring resentful thoughts about the innocent life growing inside her wasn't healthy for either of them.

"Hey," Winnie said, standing next to Skye. "I know this isn't the easiest thing in the world." Her friend turned to face her. "But I can't tell you how excited I am to have you so close. It's going to be so much fun."

"You're a…" Skye shook her head, rolling her eyes. She wanted to say her friend was a rotten trickster, but she wouldn't. Not when she knew Winnie's heart.

"I can't believe I'm doing this," Skye said, thinking there was no way she would have bet a month ago that she'd be getting married by the Justice of the Peace the last Thursday in October. Granted, the day would've been a pretty specific guess, but it wouldn't have mattered which day because she'd have still been surprised.

"Yes, *you can*, because despite your crunchy exterior, you're a softy on the inside." Winnie grinned wide.

"Crunchy?" Skye grumbled. "I'll show you crunchy."

Winnie snickered and hugged Skye around the shoulders, squeezing her. "I so do love you."

With a huff, Skye smiled. "I love you too." Didn't mean Skye wouldn't aim for the bullseye if Winnie ever found herself in a dunking booth.

Her friend held her by the shoulders as she leaned back, leveling her eyes at Skye. "Something great is going to come from this. I don't know what it is, but it's going to be wonderful. I just know it."

Optimism oozed from Winnie, and Skye had to admit she had a weird feeling her friend was right. Aside from having a baby, maybe this marriage arrangement would allow her to tuck away wisdom when it came to picking out the person she'd eventually spend the rest of her life with.

Winnie smiled. "And you deserve it. You have a kind heart and warm soul. Robert was a grade-A genuine jerk. You deserve better."

Okay, so maybe Skye was crispy on the outside and gooey in the middle. One thing was for sure: if she spoke, she'd end up in tears.

When Skye didn't reply, Winnie continued. "You don't have to go through with it if you don't want to. I don't want you to feel pressured at all."

She didn't feel that way, not really. If she were honest, she felt the opposite. Once she agreed, Bandit kept asking if she was sure. That if Skye didn't want to do it, she didn't have to because it was more than being married on paper. They were going to be living together.

She wasn't entirely positive if he was making sure she was okay or trying to get out of it himself. It's wasn't a negative thing. She understood completely. One day you're be-bopping along, and the next you're sideswiped. If nothing else, they shared that feeling.

There was also the small issue of the not-so-small amount of money he'd offered. Bandit even went so far as to give her money to pay for a lawyer so she felt secure about the contract. When she'd seen the number of zeroes, she'd nearly passed out. Over a million dollars.

She'd called Bandit immediately, asking if it was a typo, but it wasn't. He'd said she needed her bills paid, the baby needed a college fund, and if she decided she wanted to work, she'd either need daycare or a nanny. Those things weren't cheap, and if that didn't cover it, all she had to do was ask for more. That little phrase wasn't in the contract, but she had no doubt he'd honor it. He just seemed like that sort of man. Rugged, honest, and kind.

"Well," she said, looking at Winnie, "I guess it's time to get hitched." Her voice was thick, and she cleared her throat. Showing emotion in front of people was hard. Winnie wasn't just people, but strangers were going in and out of the courthouse. They had no business seeing Skye teary-eyed.

"Bandit said he'd meet us inside, that he was running a little late but I shouldn't let you stay on your feet."

Leaning back, Skye blinked. "What?" Inside, she melted. They'd talked a lot—every day since they first met and sometimes twice in a day—since she'd agreed to help, and once, in passing, she'd remarked how her feet were now beginning to swell. How had he remembered that?

Winnie shrugged. "What what?"

"Nothing." There were a billion reasons why he was being nice. They had to put up with each other for a year, and it was a smart idea to start off on a good foot.

They went inside, found the judge's office, and sat. Leaning her head against the wall, Skye hugged her purse to her stomach. This wasn't what she'd envisioned when she thought about having kids. There were no white fences involved—because she was practical and didn't want to paint that fence every year—but she'd pictured her and her husband sitting on the front porch, watching their children play.

Of course, that could still happen, but how would her baby feel? That thought had rolled around her brain the entire time she'd agreed to this marriage. Ultimately, she decided the baby would be small enough that they could transition Bandit out of the picture. Not what she wanted for him or the baby, but she also didn't want to saddle a man down with a child who wasn't his.

She rolled her head as the elevator door opened and

watched people file out of it with Bear and Bandit being the last two. He looked just as good today as he had at the restaurant. The only difference was the color of his shirt, a soft green. She'd yet to catch an eyeful of his backside, but she didn't doubt it'd rev her heart rate.

Looking to Winnie, Skye watched as her friend's gaze met Bear's. This was perhaps her favorite part of a relationship. Winnie's eyes lit up, her face flushed, and there was no mistaking the absolute adoration she felt for Bear. And Bear carried that same excitement on his face. They loved each other deeply.

Bandit stopped just as Bear did, and then Skye caught sight of what he was carrying, his hat in one hand and a bouquet in the other...and based on the small tag, they were from Skye's shop.

He stepped over to her and squatted down. "I kn-kn-know you d-d-didn't want anything f-f-fancy, but I th-thought you might like these." He dug in his shirt pocket and pulled out a ring. "I-I-I couldn't find the b-b-box for it. This w-was my grandmother's r-r-ring. I-I-I hope th-th-that's o-o-okay."

It was perhaps the simplest ring she'd ever seen. Just a plain band with a small diamond. She'd thought a billionaire would have something gaudy and over the top.

As if reading her thoughts, Bandit smiled. "My gr-gr-grandpa tried to buy my grandma a-a-another ring after they b-b-became wealthy, but she w-w-wouldn't let him. She said th-th-that nothing a-a-about their relationship had ch-ch-changed. That r-r-ring meant l-l-love and sometimes the sm-sm-smallest things s-s-speak the lo-loudest."

This man was going to give her emotional diabetes. What was there to say, though? Would she rather Bandit be like Robert? Stingy with compliments and never a nice thing to say? "That's actually very charming. I'd be happy to wear it."

The door to the judge's office opened, and a woman in a black robe looked at their small group. Peppery-flecked brown hair and crow's feet gave just a hint of her age since her skin seemed smooth and youthful—a sign she took care of it. "I'm Judge Ireland. Who's the bride and groom?"

Skye raised her hand and threw a thumb Bandit's way. "Me and this handsome devil here."

Bandit choked and used the arm of the chair to stand, then held his hand out to her. "R-r-ready?"

"Let's do this," she said, taking his hand and letting him help get her to her feet.

As soon as the judge saw Skye's belly, she looked at

Bandit with a scowl on her face. Skye could see the accusation on the woman's features.

Wrapping her arms around Bandit, she lifted her chin a fraction and held back a full-on glare. "The baby isn't his. I'm just blessed that he's wonderful enough to raise another man's child."

Bear slapped Bandit on the back. "Yep. That scoundrel she was married to found out she was pregnant and flew the coop. Rotten, horrible—"

Winnie quickly grabbed Bear's arm and clamped her hand over his mouth. "Her ex just wasn't a nice man."

Bear side-eyed her, but a smile stretched wide on his lips. Their love was equal, and they balanced each other just when it was needed. Something Skye hoped to have one day.

Still, that was entirely too much information. When the judge's features softened, it had the effect Skye wanted. One of the things she noticed about Bandit was that he typically didn't fight for himself. Something she was going to have to teach him over the next year.

"And you two are the witnesses?" The judge peered at Winnie and Bear.

"Yes, ma'am," Winnie answered as Bear nodded.

Her gaze traveled to Skye. "How far along are you?"

"Seven months." The answer was clipped.

Bandit's lips pinched together. "A-a-and I'm n-n-not leaving h-h-her either."

If Bandit really knew her, there was a chance he *would* run. That's what Robert had told her more than once. *As soon as a man gets to know you, he'll run as fast as he can. You're lucky to have me because I can put up with you.*

Sadness settled over her. She'd have to be careful with Bandit because she was already a little smitten with him, and she didn't want a relationship. Allowing her emotions to cloud her judgment was something she just couldn't do.

There *was* an out in the contract. If at any time either of them wanted to quit, they could. He'd forfeit his billions, and she'd get a third of the money. She wanted him to get his fortune, and she wanted every penny of that money. Once the marriage was over, it would give her a chance to decide what she wanted to do. So her feelings needed to mind their own business until this whole thing was over.

It was time to play the part, and if there was anything she could do, it was that. She'd force it if she had to.

CHAPTER 5

Bandit was so nervous his palms were sweating. He'd never expected to get married in a courthouse. Then again, he'd never expected to get married at all. Not that he didn't want to, but he knew his limitations.

That judge, though. Oh, he'd wanted to give her a piece of his mind. Only the way he talked, it would take him a year to do it. He never expected Skye to say anything. It was okay whatever that judge thought about him. If it had been her that woman was giving the stink eye to, that would've been another matter.

The judge waved them into her office and took her seat behind the desk. Her left eyebrow hooked upward as she looked at Bandit. "And you're sure you don't mind being this baby's father? You can't change your mind down the road. It's a baby, not a pet fish."

Now that Skye was becoming Mrs. Ochoa, she was his priority—fake marriage or not. While living with his grandpa, their talks had shaped what he thought about life even more, especially their conversations about marriage. It was a two-way street and a heap of work, but Skye was the one being inconvenienced, not him. She was free to do as she pleased without any comments or expectations from him.

His lips pinched together along with his eyebrows. This judge was a pill. "I-I-I know. I-I-I'm not changing m-m-my m-m-mind. Th-th-this baby w-w-will be m-m-mine the rest of h-h-his life. I d-d-don't walk out on my ch-ch-children."

It wasn't until after he spoke that he realized Skye might not appreciate that claim. He bowed his head, keeping his eyes from fully meeting hers. "S-s-sorry."

Cupping his face, she pressed a kiss to his cheek. "It's okay. It came from a good place."

Boy, that tiny kiss sure packed a punch. For a second, he wondered what a real one would feel like... and then his brain clicked on. He didn't need to be thinking about Skye like that. She was only marrying him so her child would be cared for. That's all. They had to sell this thing to the judge. If she realized it was a fake marriage, she might not be willing to perform it.

Skye dropped her hand and turned to the woman. "He's a special man; that's for sure."

Judge Ireland's lips formed a hard line as she nodded. "Yes, must be." Her gaze flicked from Bandit to Skye a few times. "I've married too many couples only to find they've divorced later, and I don't like it."

Bandit suspected that could weigh heavily on someone, but it wasn't her business. He wasn't doing this by choice. Not only did his grandpa's finances demand it, but now he'd made a promise to Skye too. He couldn't back out.

"Why do the two of you think you should be married?" the judge asked.

His heart rate jumped. This wasn't a question he'd expected. Of course, he'd spoken to Skye a lot over the last month and a half. They needed to get a little familiar with each other since they'd be living together.

"He took care of his ill grandpa for a year before the man passed away. A man he hardly knew in the beginning." Skye held herself a little higher. "He's done sweet things for me like…" She smiled as her gaze fell to the flowers he'd brought her. "He's done things like sent me groceries when I didn't feel good. Even when he told the delivery boy not to mention names, I knew it was him. He's just an all-around good man. Those are hard to find."

Shoot. Bandit didn't want her to know he'd sent the groceries. She'd told him not to do it, but he'd heard the exhaustion in her voice and hated it. Being pregnant wasn't easy on a woman's body, and she needed those groceries.

He looked at her, his already-racing pulse jumping higher. "Sh-she's the prettiest w-w-woman I've ever met. Wh-wh-when I...d-d-don't stick up for m-m-myself, she's a w-w-warrior."

The longer he held her gaze, the quieter the world became. All the clutter and chaos in his mind settled as he found himself falling deeper into those dark pools. "Plus, she had a lot of options when she found out she was pregnant. It took a lot of courage to keep the baby. I can't help but admire that."

Tears pooled in her eyes before she leaned her head against his shoulder. "Thank you."

The spell he'd been under was broken, and he realized he'd said all that in front of everyone. He also recognized a look of shock on Bear's and Winnie's faces. He'd spoken clearly for the first time in front of someone. Getting lost in a beautiful woman's eyes was a sure-fire way to have that happen. He could almost hear his grandpa saying it.

The judge's expression lifted. "Well, at least this time I've got a couple I can have faith in."

Bandit held back a flinch. He hated lying to this judge.

She pointed her finger at Skye. "You're right. He's one of the hard-to-find good men. You hang on to him."

"Yes, ma'am," Skye replied. Of course, she only said that for the judge's benefit. Bandit knew that.

"And you," she said, turning that finger onto Bandit. "You've got a special lady right here. One that fights for you and makes tough decisions."

Bandit nodded. "Yes, ma'am."

"Remember what you said in my chambers when you're experiencing hard times." Judge Ireland stood and clasped her hands in front of her. "Okay, have we got rings?"

"Got mine." She dug into the dress pocket.

He'd told her she didn't need to worry about it.

A sly smile quirked on her lips. "Took me a few days, but I found the perfect one."

Days? He wanted to say it wasn't necessary, but the judge was listening, so he wouldn't comment on that.

"I h-h-have hers t-t-too." He held up the tiny ring his grandpa had given his grandma.

He'd given it to Bandit long before his passing. It was the thing that led to all their discussions about life, marriage, and everything in between. That's probably where Bandit's grandpa got this wild idea to force Bandit to marry. Bandit had said he didn't see a future where he had a wife and children.

Oh, that'd been a blowout. Their only fight the entire time Bandit lived there. His grandpa chewed him to pieces. He had no business thinking he wasn't worthy of being loved. That his sorry-behind son had no right telling Bandit it was his fault he was leaving. Little did Bandit know his grandpa would remember that incident and take action.

Judge Ireland dove right into the ceremony. The vows on Bandit's part were easy. He didn't mind pledging loyalty and honor to her. His only regret was that he'd have to end it in a year. Granted, he didn't know her as well as he hoped he eventually would, but he had a feeling she was a woman worth all the promises he could make.

Announcing them as husband and wife squeezed his heart a little too tightly. The gravity of the situation was always present, but right then, the ramification hit him square in the chest. He was a married man, and he took that responsibility seriously. Fake or not.

"Well, I bet this is the part you two have been waiting on the most," the judge said. "You can kiss your bride, Mr. Ochoa."

His breath caught. Why hadn't he thought about this part? He was so focused on making sure Skye was okay with their arrangement that it never even crossed his mind. He'd been to enough weddings the last few years that it should've been front and center.

Turning to Skye, he said, "We—"

Before he could get a full word out, she took his face in her hands and pressed her lips to his. His cheek still needed medical attention from the last kiss. How was he going to eat with scorched lips?

They were trying to make a judge believe they were truly married, except this kiss didn't feel so fake. Not for him. He liked Skye from the moment he met her. There was something about her that grabbed him, and over the last month and a half, talking to her, claws had sunk deep into him.

This kiss she was laying on him wasn't helping those claws retract at all. The longer her lips stayed connected to his, the harder his heart hammered in his chest. His arms slid around her waist, pulling her closer. He knew this was a show for the judge, but he couldn't stop himself from responding. The feel of her lips, the way her belly pressed against him, all of it made for a heady experience and one he wouldn't mind happening often.

At the clearing of someone's throat, Skye pulled away. In all Bandit's years of living through Caprock winters, he'd never felt as cold as he did right that second. If he could've gotten away with it, he'd have held her endlessly to stave off the whisper of winter that shimmied down his spine.

The one thing he didn't miss was the dazed look in Skye's dark eyes. He quickly dismissed the thought as something he'd wanted to see and not reality. Still, if that was the only kiss he ever shared with her, he'd wrap that memory in a box and hide it in his mind. A horrible thought since he'd be comparing any future kiss with this one.

Winnie fanned herself. "Wow." She looked at Bear. "Did we look like that on our wedding day?"

A blush crept into Bear's cheeks, and he shrugged. "I don't know. You wanna recreate it and have the judge decide?"

She popped him on the bicep. "No, you…"

He pulled her against. "You what?"

"Frustrating man."

"I wouldn't be nearly as frustrating if you didn't love me so much." He winked.

Winnie's face gave her hair competition for which might be more crimson. Instead of responding, she huffed and gave him a quick kiss. "There might be some truth in that."

Judge Ireland chuckled. "Over the years, I've had countless couples in my office. I know life has a way of testing people, and that can wear on you. It's weathered my soul, and you four just breathed life into it."

Bandit may as well have stolen gum for as wretched as he felt. He'd lied to this woman. An act that cut him to the quick. Skye had signed a year-long contract, but maybe he could treat her well enough that she'd want to stick around. Although, it made his heart hurt when thinking it. He wasn't sure he could have more than that, but it didn't stop him from wanting it.

Skye nodded and smiled. "Yep. That's me. Restoring faith in relationships with a single kiss." Her humor was dry, and most took it as her being aloof or stand-offish. Those were her shields. She used them to protect herself much like he used retreating from people. It was better to let people forget he existed rather than fight to be seen.

"Well," she turned to Bandit, "I don't know about

you, but I'm hungry. You want to grab a bite to eat? The movers aren't supposed to be there for a few more hours."

"H-h-how about I t-t-take you home and m-m-make you something? That way you can prop your feet up." He grinned.

She eyed him a second. "Are you trying to say my ankles are fat?"

His mouth dropped open as his brain screamed, *Danger!* "N-no, I-I-I d-didn't m-m-mean..." He clamped his lips shut, closing his eyes.

A warm palm came to rest on his cheek. "Look at me."

"I..."

"Bandit." Sky's voice was soft.

He opened his eyes, waiting for a lecture, but what he saw wasn't anything he expected.

Her lips quirked up in one corner. "I was kidding. Home sounds nice, and the feet part especially so." Skye's hand dropped to her side, and she smiled, linking her arm with his. "Take me home, cowboy."

She was playing up the relationship for the judge, and he knew that. Once they were out of Judge Ireland's chambers, they'd go back to the platonic-friend thing they'd agreed upon. "Yes, m-m-ma'am."

The next year wouldn't be dull; that's for sure. He'd

just have to remember that neither of them wanted anything more than friendship. Her more so than him, and he wasn't going to push her one bit. She needed a friend right now, and if that's all she wanted, well, he'd oblige. It was the honorable thing to do.

CHAPTER 6

A sigh poured from Skye, and with it, the apprehension of the day's events so far. Once they'd reached Bandit's little cabin, she'd been given a tour of the place. It was humble, cozy, and comforting. If she had to give the place a style, it would be Bandit —simple, accommodating, and easy. She'd never seen a home fit its occupants as perfectly as this one.

The biggest surprise was her bedroom. She had no idea how he'd done it so quickly, but he'd gone to the trouble of remodeling the attached bathroom. Plus, it had been done in colors she'd mentioned here and there with décor that fit her. She didn't think the year would be torture anyway, but the effort he'd put in spoke to her heart.

"It's like there was a foot switch when I hit four

months. They're swelling when I've barely done anything." Totally true. One day she was fine, and the next, *wham*, elephant ankles.

Bandit shot her a look over his shoulder where he was standing at the stove. "I-I-I'm s-s-sorry." He'd been extra quiet since they left Amarillo, which bothered her. He seemed to carry his stuttering like a curse. It wasn't, and it didn't lessen him as a man. He was thoughtful, kind, and caring. She'd take that over an overbearing Robert any day.

He'd been nothing but sweet to her since she met him. Which explained the kiss at the courthouse. Her emotions were battered and bruised at the moment. Of course she'd find that type of man attractive. That didn't change anything about her availability.

Not only was Skye not looking for a relationship, but even Bandit had mentioned as much a few times. Her reasons were sound, though, after her marriage failed so quickly. She needed a little time to get her feet under her and find out what she wanted to do before dragging a man into the picture.

"That sure smells good," she said.

He'd pulled out two thick steaks, mashed some potatoes, and sautéed some broccoli. If it tasted as good as it smelled, she'd lick the bowls clean.

Grunting a laugh, he pulled plates from the

cupboard, plated some food, and set one of the dishes in front of her. "I-I-I hope y-y-you like it."

Bandit took a seat across from her, keeping his gaze pinned on his food. He bowed his head, and a short murmur of prayer was sent heavenward. Skye was touched by it. It'd been one of her family's traditions as she was growing up. A family meal, a prayer, and then talking about the day to keep them connected.

The lingering silence stretched between them as they each dug into their meal. Winnie could cook. That woman was amazing in a kitchen, but Bandit tied her abilities. The steak was fork-tender, the mashed potatoes were smooth with a buttery flavor and perfectly seasoned, and the salad tasted crisp and fresh. She didn't even like salad.

Halfway through her meal, she set her fork down. "This is some of the best food I've ever eaten. Why didn't you ever open a restaurant? Or work with Winnie?"

Keeping his head down, he said, "Oh, w-w-well, there's l-l-lots of talking involved and..." He let the sentence die.

If it was the last thing she did, she'd find a way to help him with that. She couldn't understand why he was so nervous around people. He wasn't one of those types who came off as naturally prickly. It didn't make sense. "Have you always stuttered?"

He gave her a small shrug. "I-I-I don't remember."

The desire to push him was on the tip of her tongue, but she didn't want to alienate him either. "Okay." They needed to know each other better before she went down that path.

What better way than to make conversation while they ate? "So, how did you get the bathroom done so quickly? It looks practically new."

"It *is* n-n-new." His gaze darted from his plate to her and back down.

"New as in just a fresh coat of paint...or?" Surely he wasn't saying he'd had that bathroom built. Yes, he *would* be a billionaire, but that would be too much. There was also the matter that he'd have to be married a year to pay for it.

With a small shrug, he replied, "New. I h-h-had it built for y-y-you." He paused. "I b-b-borrowed it from Bear w-w-with the promise I'll p-p-pay it back."

Skye's jaw was hanging low enough she could almost feel the gravy on her chin. "Built? You mean..." She swallowed hard while her mind tripped over itself to catch up.

"I didn't w-w-want you to f-f-feel uncomfortable.

I-I-I want you to feel s-s-safe and warm and...protected."

She leaned forward. "You did that for me?" Her brain felt squishy. Robert had never done anything remotely like that. Not that he could afford to build a bathroom, but to put her needs anywhere on his list at all. "And you borrowed the money? I didn't realize..." It never even crossed her mind he'd do something like that for her. "I don't need to snoop in your finances."

He lifted his head, catching her gaze and holding it. "Sure you d-d-do. I know th-th-this isn't a real marriage," he said, pulling his gaze away from hers before finishing the sentence. "B-b-but you have a st-st-stake in me keeping m-m-my grandpa's fortune. You n-n-need to know what I'm d-d-doing with the money." His voice grew soft.

Skye had no idea what to think of Bandit. Of course, she'd thought he was pretty wonderful to begin with, but this took things to a new level. He had to be putting up a front for her. Men like him just didn't exist. She should know since she'd dated her fair share of losers and then gone and married one.

Before she could respond, a knock came from the door. Bandit stood and smiled. "Are y-y-you feeling okay?"

She blinked. "Yes, why?"

"Because th-th-that knock would be the Wests c-c-coming to pay a v-v-visit. I d-d-don't want to l-l-let them in unless y-y-you're feeling up to-to-to it."

With a snort, she stood. "Oh, well, let's rip that bandage off."

One of their conversations had centered around their families. She'd told him about her mom and dad and all about her siblings and the Santa's-list size of aunts, uncles, and cousins. She'd felt a little bad for Bandit when he only spoke of his mom as he was growing up. It was difficult to imagine life without her huge family.

When they reached the door full of Wests, her sympathy dissipated a little. Of course, she knew Bear and Winnie. She figured they were there just to give her a couple of friendly faces in the crowd.

The introductions were almost too quick for Skye. Trying to keep all the names with the right faces seemed impossible—and this didn't include two of the brothers, Hunter and Josiah, who lived elsewhere with their wives and children. Winnie had often talked about the family, and meeting them in person, they were as she described—warm, friendly, and welcoming. They'd left their children with Gabby's parents while they visited.

"So, you've lived your entire life in Amarillo?"

asked Caroline, Bear's mother, as she sat next to her husband.

"Yes, ma'am," Skye replied.

Caroline waved her off. "Call me Caroline, please."

Winnie chuckled and smiled. "Don't argue. You won't win."

"That's right." Caroline leaned against her husband, King.

He winked at her and grinned. "Same goes for me. Only, use King, please."

"Bandit said you were expecting." Caroline phrased the statement more like a question.

"Yes, ma'am—Caroline. I'm seven months along."

Her grin widened. "Another grandbaby." The woman seemed almost giddy, which in turn only made Skye like the family more.

"Mom, you're going to scare the poor woman," said Wyatt, one of Bear's brothers.

"Hush, Wyatt!" Caroline glanced at him before returning her attention to Skye. "Don't listen to him."

Carrie Anne, the West brothers' only sister, snickered. "She's got baby on the brain."

It was easy to see why Bandit loved the Wests. They were more than just warm and friendly. It was like once they met someone, that person belonged to them.

Skye's family was somewhat like that but with a bit of a critical streak that didn't seem to run in this group. So far, she felt nothing in the way of judgment coming from them. If only she could say *that* of her family. Once she decided to marry Bandit, she'd gone to her mom and dad and told them about the pregnancy and the marriage. It took every bit of her self-control to hide the shiver that raced down her spine as she recalled that day.

Just the memory of the conversation made her stomach roil. Her mom had been furious while her dad was disappointed. Once the initial shock wore off, they'd offered to help. Well, her dad had. More likely he'd talked her mom into it. Because of that, it felt less than genuine, and Skye had turned down their offer.

After telling her mom and dad, she'd made the calls to her sister and brother as well. The holidays were coming up, and she didn't want to be introducing her siblings to her husband for the first time.

"Have you thought of names?" Gabby asked.

Winnie had spoken of that relationship before. Wyatt and Gabby were childhood friends who fell in love. There was no denying the devotion either. They were meant for each other, and it was obvious.

A tiny pang of want flitted through Skye's heart. Now that she was examining her relationship with

Robert, it was pretty obvious that she'd loved him and accepted what pittance he'd offered as all she deserved. She was blunt, spoke her mind...she was exactly what Winnie said: crunchy. The soft interior was debatable, though.

Skye smiled. "Not really..." She winced. "I don't really want to know what I'm having until they're here."

Caroline's mouth dropped open. "Well, that would certainly add some excitement."

"It doesn't bother you?" The question popped out quicker than Skye could rein it in. Her mom had hated the idea. How would she know what to buy if she didn't know whether Skye was having a boy or girl?

"Oh, no. Why would it bother me? We'll just have to figure out what neutral color you like. Sage-green is pretty, and so is soft-blue. Oh, gosh, so many ways to decorate. It'll be fun."

We. The word made Skye's heart bubble. Until she remembered that these folks loved Bandit and knew all about the marriage. Still, it was nice to have some support even if it wasn't totally for her.

"We should take some measurements. The next time we go into town, we can get a few things." Caroline turned to Gabby. "How have you liked the crib you have?"

"I love it. It's one of those convertible ones." She smiled as she looked at Skye. "Travis loves thinking he's sleeping in a big-boy bed."

Now that furniture was brought up, Skye realized that was one aspect of her pregnancy she hadn't considered. Then it dawned on her why her room was so large. Bandit had done it on purpose, so she had room for the baby. As discreetly as she could, she looked at him—appreciating him as a person.

"I hadn't even thought of that, to be honest," Skye said. "I guess I do need to start figuring all that out."

Carrie Anne shrugged. "Don't stress. You've got plenty of time."

"That's right," Caroline said. "No pressure at all."

"What are y'all doing for Christmas, Bandit?" asked King. "You two staying here or going to Amarillo?"

Bandit looked startled, but Skye couldn't blame him. She hadn't thought about that either. More than likely, her parents would want them to make some sort of appearance.

"I-I-I hadn't thought ab-b-bout it." Bandit looked to Skye. "We'll d-d-do whatever sh-she wants to do."

Another stark difference between Robert and Bandit. Bandit was looking to her for help with decisions instead of just barking orders. To be fair, her family hadn't really welcomed Robert with open arms.

It'd been more like an oil-and-water situation. Mostly, it was Skye in the middle, feeling uncomfortable and ready to leave before whatever family function had even started.

Skye sighed. "We'll probably need to plan a visit. They don't do anything super special. Typically, we meet at a restaurant and have lunch or dinner. It's pretty low-key, really."

Carrie Anne laughed. "That actually doesn't sound bad at all."

Shaking his head, Bear replied, "Our traditions are just fine."

"What he means to say is that he loves everyone staying at the house during Thanksgiving and Christmas, and he'd miss you if you didn't." Winnie bumped her shoulder against Bear. "Right?"

Slowly, a smile quirked on the man's lips. He leaned down and gave her a quick kiss. "You're right a lot."

Another thing that Skye wanted. The comfortableness that Bear and Winnie had. They'd had that from the first time Skye met them. It was another trait Skye was putting on her mental list of things she wanted whenever she did settle down with someone.

If nothing else, she got the impression that by the time her contract with Bandit was up, she'd have a full list of expectations and a bar set for her heart that she wouldn't lower. Either the guy would meet it or she'd call it done. There wouldn't be a second Robert, especially now that she was not only protecting herself but her baby too. The next guy would be the right guy, or she wouldn't have one at all.

The moment the thought ran through her head, her gaze landed on Bandit and her heart skipped a beat. It needed to cut that out. They had a contract, and her track record with men was still suspect. At the end of the year, she'd move on. That's all there was to it.

CHAPTER 7

With a loud sigh, Bandit shut the door after the last West walked out. In true Texas fashion, there had been at least ten rounds of goodbyes, and if *he* was tired, he was positive Skye was.

Of course, plans were made for the next get-together before they left. They arranged that the Wests would meet them in two days for the Saturday Farmer's Market at Wyatt and Gabby's place.

Since starting it a few years ago, it had taken off. With the cattle ranch thriving again, jobs were being filled not only there but in other areas too. The tiny town they called home seemed to be revitalized, and they were all happy to see it. Caprock Canyon was a good place to live and raise a family.

"Well, they're certainly an adventure, huh?" Skye asked, chuckling.

"I l-l-love them, b-b-but they can be a bit m-m-much for people who d-d-don't know them." He pushed off the door and walked to the table, picking up the remains of his and Skye's lunch. Before he could get too far with them, Skye snatched her plate from him.

Popping open the microwave door, she smiled. "Second lunch."

He winced and quickly strode the few feet to the microwave. "Th-th-that's not how you r-r-reheat food." He'd only used that thing for popcorn and even then, only in times of dire need. Food just didn't come out tasting right.

She slapped the door shut and stood in front of it. "No, but it's the fastest way."

"Oh, come on n-n-now. Y-y-you're gonna r-r-ruin it."

"That just means it'll taste like a mortal man prepared it. I'm okay with that." Her lips quirked up at the corners. Man, she was cute.

"It's not the f-f-fastest w-w-way, but the oven is b-b-better." His gaze dipped to his plate, and his stomach gave a small growl. The Wests had interrupted their meal, and now that he was thinking about it, he was still a little hungry.

Skye laughed. "Okay, then. You do yours that way, and I'll do mine this way. We'll have a taste test."

"Fine." He walked to the drawer with the foil in it, pulled off a sheet, and wrapped his plate before setting it in the oven and hitting bake. "Mine'll b-b-be better."

"Care to make a wager?" She crossed her arms over her chest and narrowed her eyes.

Bandit wasn't sure what he liked the most about her, her feistiness or her determination. He settled on both since there really wasn't a need for a first place. So far, there wasn't much he *didn't* like about her. Put on the spot, he wouldn't be able to really name anything he'd call a deal-breaker. They'd only been together a few hours, which didn't give them near enough time to get on each other's nerves.

"Wh-wh-what sort of wager?"

Like she'd not thought through the offer of a bet, her lips pursed and she looked at the floor. When she lifted her gaze to his again, the sparkle nearly knocked him over. No one on earth could say the woman wasn't drop-dead gorgeous to begin with, but those eyes were beyond simple words. "Cinnamon rolls."

He tilted his head. "That's all?"

The glint in her eyes shone a little brighter, and she spun in place, quickly punching in a minute on the timer and turning back to him. "Have you got other things up those sleeves of yours? Because what I've been told about those rolls is it's heaven in my mouth." As fast as the change in the West Texas weather, her shoulders sagged. "I don't really need the cinnamon rolls, though," she said, pinching her sides and wiggling it. "I've got enough blubber to survive a snowstorm in the Antarctic."

What? Blubber? Taking her by the shoulders, he took a step closer. "Don't you ever say anything like that again. You are a beautiful woman with the prettiest hair and eyes I've ever seen. Anyone who says otherwise is just plain...well, stupid."

Water welled in her eyes. "You think I'm beautiful?"

"Well, of course I do. What man wouldn't?" It was then he realized he'd made a mistake by stepping closer. If he didn't back away quickly, he wouldn't be able to stave off the temptation to kiss her. Dropping his hands from her shoulders, he stepped back. "I can't imagine anyone thinking anything differently."

He also realized he hadn't stuttered. It seemed when it came to her, he wasn't sure what to expect when his mouth was moving. It was either barely able to speak or the words flowing so smoothly they didn't want to stop. If only he could figure out how to do it all the time.

She half turned from him. "My ex…he…he didn't like how I looked. He always told me I needed to watch my weight." She shrugged. "It wasn't just him, though. My sister is a toothpick, and I've been compared to her since I was born."

The hurt in her voice laced every word, and it broke his heart to hear it. No, this marriage wasn't real, but the vows were, and as long as they were in this agreement, he'd hold up his end of those vows. "I'll s-s-say nothing ill about a-a-any of them, but th-th-they're wrong. You're b-b-beautiful."

With a sniff, she waved him off. "I think these pregnancy hormones are getting the better of me." Her lips lifted into a wide smile, but he could still see the hurt in her eyes. She was used to people hurting her. Maybe by the time they parted, she'd expect more than pain from people.

She caught her lip in her teeth. "You know I caught that you didn't stutter, right?"

Bandit scratched the back of his neck, his gaze dipping to the floor as heart rushed into his cheeks and raced to the tips of his ears. "I-I-I suspected y-y-you d-d-did." If there were a tire nearby, he'd kick it.

His stupid tongue just couldn't, or wouldn't, work right.

"Okay, just wanted to make you aware of it."

The lilt in her voice made him jerk his gaze to hers, and silence stretched almost uncomfortably. The ding of the microwave burst the bubble of tension, and whatever held them in place was gone. She smiled. "You never said what you wanted if you won."

"I don't know. Don't really need anything." He held up his hands as she started to argue. "Let me think on it."

She lips jutted out in a pout. "All right."

Clearing his throat, Bandit looked at the oven. "I have a few more minutes to get mine hot."

With a small prance, she floated over to the table and sat. "It better hurry up, or I'll have to nuke mine again." The laughter coating the words weren't missed by him.

"Y-y-you're a little c-c-competitive, huh?" He laughed.

"When the world's best cinnamon rolls are hanging in the balance, can you blame me?" She punctuated the question by scooping up a forkful of food and eating it.

Shaking his head, he turned from her, but he couldn't stop the smile from forming on his lips. What she didn't know was that it didn't matter who won; she was getting those cinnamon rolls.

Once his meal was heated enough, he used a couple of oven mitts to pull it from the oven and headed to the table with it. Now that he was looking at Skye's plate, her food looked a tinge gray.

Steam rolled off his plate the second he pulled the foil from it. Reheating had taken some of the color from the veggies, but not enough that they looked like they needed medical attention. "If c-c-color is an indication, m-m-mine wins."

"No way. They look the same."

He leveled his eyes at her. "N-n-not even close."

They held each other's gaze a second before she stabbed a piece of his broccoli and popped it into her mouth. Fanning her mouth, she squeaked, "Hot!" As it cooled, she chewed a little slower.

Taking his cue from her, he swiped a stalk of hers and chewed it, quickly spitting it out in his napkin. "M-m-mushy." Next, he tried his own, and the crispness wasn't as great as when it was first served, but it still had a bite unlike hers. "Mine wins that one."

Her eyes narrowed. "Maybe."

They did the meat and potatoes the same way, taking a bite from each other's plate. The potatoes were pretty much even, but the steak on his plate won.

It was way more tender than that nuked thing Skye had.

Once she finished chewing the piece of steak in her mouth, she said, "Fine, you win." The words came out begrudgingly as she sighed. "I kinda ruined it."

Without a moment's hesitation, he slid his plate across the table until his was touching hers. "H-h-here. You take m-m-mine." He gripped her plate, and her hand snaked out to stop him.

"That's not fair. You were right. It's not right that I take yours."

"You g-g-go on ahead. I-I-I wasn't h-h-hungry, r-r-really. Honestly, I'm ready f-f-for a nap. As s-s-soon as I d-d-do the dishes, I'm p-p-planning on a n-n-nap."

"It's still not fair," she replied, holding his gaze. "I know you're still hungry."

With his free hand, he patted the top of hers and pulled away with her plate. "Y-y-you go ahead. I'll be f-f-fine." He stood, taking her plate to the sink and raking the contents into the trash before washing it.

By the time he was done, she'd finished and walked to him. "Thank you."

Silence stretched a moment like she wanted to say more. Instead, she used her body to move him over and washed her plate and the silverware. "I really don't need the cinnamon rolls. I think waiting until

Christmas Eve will make them more special." She nodded toward his bedroom. "You go take a nap, and I'll finish up here. Maybe you'll know what you want for winning when you wake up."

He started to protest, and she held up her hand. "No arguing."

Smiling, he nodded. "Okay."

As he turned, she hugged him around the chest. "I do appreciate everything. I just don't know how to say a proper thank you."

The hug she was giving him might as well have been pure gold as far as he was concerned.

Wrapping his arms around her, he planted a kiss on the top of her head like it was the most natural thing in the world. "Th-th-this'll do. I o-o-owe you thanks too."

Time seemed to pause a moment while they stood there. At least, to Bandit it did. If it were up to him, he'd just stay like that. He'd practically just met her, but he could easily see a future with her. Only, this was make-believe, and at the end of the year, she'd be gone.

At the thought, a chunk of his heart broke off. She deserved better than him, and she had to know it. This was only her thanking him for the little he'd done to make things comfortable for her.

He slowly pulled away and smiled. By the time this was over, he was going to be a hulled-out mess. Skye Alvarez would be an easy woman to fall for, and he didn't have that luxury. She needed to be free to find a man who could see all the good things she had to offer. One who could talk. Plus, she had a florist shop in Amarillo to return to. Why would she stay on a ranch in the middle of nowhere with a fella like Bandit?

Even if Bandit had a silken tongue, it didn't matter. She wasn't looking for a relationship. She had the baby to think of, and she'd told him matter-of-factly that she wasn't dating anyone until the baby was old enough to understand. And she'd never offered an age for when that would be. He'd promised to respect that from the get-go, and he wasn't about to break a promise to her. When it came time to part, he'd be there for her as a friend. No matter how hard it was.

CHAPTER 8

S itting on the edge of the bed, Skye braced her arms on her knees. It wasn't the bed keeping her awake. The little toot in her tummy was in an MMA match with her kidney, and comfort was nowhere in sight.

Another kick, and she palmed her stomach. "Little person, it's rude to hit your mother." As if in a parting shot, a hand or foot smacked her outstretched palm. "You know being hardheaded doesn't make things in life easy." A snort popped out. Well, at least she'd be particularly equipped to handle such a mindset.

She took a deep breath, and the scent of something baking filled her nose. What an odd thing to smell in the middle of the night. Grabbing her phone, she checked the time. Yep, three in the morning definitely qualified as middle of the night. With a grunt, she stood, crossed the room, and cracked open the door.

The heavenly aroma of yeast and cinnamon hit her full force, and little invisible fingers hooked onto the end of her nose, pulling her forward to the source of whatever was making her mouth water. Stopping at the kitchen doorway, she looked on in awe as Bandit stood over one of the counters covered in flour and rolled-out dough.

"Why are you up so late?" she asked.

Bandit startled and nearly dropped the rolling pin before spinning to face her. "Lord have mercy, you scared me."

It wasn't funny. She'd obviously caught him off guard, but knowing it was awful to laugh didn't stop it at all. "I'm so sorry. I'm not laughing at you. I promise."

"Are too," he grumbled and turned back to the counter. "The one in the oven is almost done, and I'm almost done with this one."

"Two pans of rolls? How many do you think I'm going to eat?" He was putting his rolls where his mouth was when it came to her weight. Yeah, she was eating for two, but with the way she'd been sucking down food lately, it was more like two hundred.

Bandit didn't seem to care about that. At least,

that's what she saw in his eyes when he held her shoulders and told her she was beautiful. It was in the forcefulness of his words too. He meant every word, and she knew it. Well, she tried to know it.

As many times as Robert and her family reminded her of her weight, it was hard to believe anything else. She'd been overweight by a good forty pounds before getting pregnant. If Robert were still in the picture, there's no telling what he'd say. Probably that she needed to eat less to make sure the baby didn't come out fat too. Her mom wasn't much better. Of course, they were just little side remarks, but they still stung. Her dad and siblings didn't seem to care as long as Skye was happy.

Bandit offered a shrug as he shot her a look over his shoulder. "I'd be in trouble if I made you some and didn't make Carrie Anne a few."

"You know that's three times now that you haven't stuttered." She was hoping by making him aware of it that he'd realize he didn't have to be nervous when they were alone together.

A slight nod was all she got in response. Crossing the room, she stopped next to him. "So, what all goes into making cinnamon rolls?"

He pursed his lips and tipped his chin to a wrinkled, barely legible piece of paper with feminine hand-writing.

"There's always more to a recipe than just the ingredients." She bumped him with her shoulder, hoping to loosen his tongue again.

Again, he nodded and continued working on the rolls.

Covering his hand with hers, she said, "Bandit, you have no reason to be nervous around me. We're going to be living together for the next year."

His eyes closed, and it seemed he clamped his lips together even tighter.

Okay, the sweet approach didn't work. She took her hand from his and took his chin in her fingers. "Bandit. Look at me."

Instead of opening his eyes, he tried to pull away.

Okay, now she was getting upset. "Bandit."

Nothing.

Struck with determination, she squeezed herself between him and the counter. "Christopher Ochoa, you look at me right this second!"

His eyes flew open. "No one calls me that."

"Gotcha to open your eyes, didn't it?" She smiled.

He sucked in a lungful of air, his shoulders rounding. "I…"

This time she took his face in her hands. "I know

this marriage is fake, but our friendship doesn't have to be. You don't stutter when you're alone, do you?"

"N..." He sighed. "No."

"Then it's not fair for me to invade the one place you feel safe and take that away from you. I certainly can use the money, but I'll move out tomorrow if you're that nervous around me. I'll not carry the weight of knowing I'm causing you that much distress by staying here. It would be wrong of me to stay."

His mouth parted slightly.

"I mean it." She squared her shoulders. Yep, she needed the money desperately, and since he'd already given her some, she'd owe him, but she wouldn't make him live a year like this. "I just can't do that to you. You've been so kind to me, and to take away the one place you feel safe and secure just isn't right."

Slowly, his posture softened, and he nodded. "Okay. I...I'll try." He worked a little too hard to get it out, but it was a solid sentence.

"From the bottom of my heart, I don't care that you stutter. It doesn't change my opinion of you one bit. You're a wonderful man." She dropped her hands to her sides. "I just don't want to be the cause of your stress. I'd feel terrible, and we're friends, right?" Hopefully, by the end of the year, he wouldn't have trouble at all, but she'd keep that little goal to herself. This deal they were making was enough pushing for one night.

"Skye...I just..."

"You just did it. You've been doing it when you don't think about it. Stop thinking about it. Stop over-analyzing. From what I could tell of the Wests, they'd accept a monkey with a clubbed foot if they loved it. I'm not saying they've got low standards. I'm saying they love freely and wholly, and it's easy to see that they love *you*. I've never felt more comfortable being around a group of people in my life."

The truest statement ever spoken. They'd made her feel like she was a member of the family in less than thirty minutes after arriving. Bandit wasn't even blood, but if she hadn't known, she'd have never guessed it by the way the Wests treated Bandit.

"It's easier said than done." The words were clipped, but not out of anger. He was pulling tooth and nail to speak clearly.

"I know, but you aren't someone who gives up easily. I may not have known you long, but that is one trait I picked up on right away." She caught his gaze and held it, trying to will him to understand that she liked him. If she hadn't, she never would've agreed to marry him. Fake or not, there was only so much money a person would take to deal with a cantankerous person.

Bandit inhaled and let it out slowly. "Do you really want to know how to make cinnamon rolls?" he asked, still forcing the words out but easier than the last time.

"Yes, but fair warning, I burn things like my name should be Pyro." She laughed. "I can almost look at a stove and it'll burst into flames."

Chuckling, he smiled, and the corners of his eyes crinkled. Another thing about him that Skye liked. She could tell he was a generally happy person by those little lines that had already accumulated there. Something she should have paid more attention to when it came to Robert.

"I've got a fire extinguisher in the panty over there. I think we'll be okay," he said, moving to the side to make room for her at the counter.

His words were tight and controlled, but she was okay with that. She wasn't expecting he'd be a golden-tongued orator overnight, but it was a step in the right direction. That's what mattered.

Over the next hour, he explained how to put everything together slowly and with more patience than she'd ever experienced. It was as labor-intensive as she'd expected. First, making the dough, then rolling it out, and then slathering on the cinnamon mixture before rolling it up and cutting it.

When the timer went off, he opened the oven door to pull out the tray and slide the next in. The hot rolls smelled good before, but now, with nothing between them and her, it was magical.

Once the icing was drizzled over them, he plated one and handed it to her. The steam trailed behind her as she walked to the table and sat. She knew it was screaming hot, but she couldn't stop herself from pinching off a piece and popping it into her mouth.

A moan spilled out of her from a place so deep it almost sounded alien to her. "Oh my word, Bandit."

Who needed millions of dollars to live with this man when he could cook things that Jesus must have whispered in his ear? Of course, cinnamon rolls wouldn't pay her bills, but there was a tiny part of her that wouldn't mind homelessness if these were a promised daily offering.

"This has to be the best thing I've ever put in my mouth." That was saying a lot, too, because Winnie's crème brûlée was the best thing she'd ever eaten until now. She pulled off a larger piece and bit into it. "I have to owe you for making these," she said, holding her hand over her mouth as she lifted her gaze to his.

A smile graced his lips. "Naw, I just got my payment."

Her cheeks had to be hotter than the fresh-from-the-oven roll. She waved him off. "Oh, stop." She broke off more of the roll, keeping her eyes on her plate as she ate it. "Are you going to have one?"

"No, I'm okay."

She sighed heavily. That was just like something Robert would do. Tell her she needed to lose weight and then ask her if she wanted to go for ice cream. She was pulled in two all the time. If she said she didn't want ice cream, he'd get mad that she was keeping him from having fun. Except, he'd get something tiny or low-fat. Skye was allergic to most artificial sweeteners, and they tasted funny to her. Even if she got a small one, though, she'd get looks from Robert like she should've just come with him and abstained from getting a treat.

Pushing the half-eaten roll away, she stood. "I'm good too."

Before she could get two steps away, Bandit had her by the hand, pulling her to a stop. "What just happened?" Their eyes locked as he seemed to search hers, desperate for an answer.

"Nothing. I'm tired." She forced a smile and shook her head.

His posture softened as he held her gaze. "Come on, Skye."

She didn't want to hurt Bandit nor mess up the progress they'd made with his speech, but she couldn't handle this conversation right now and keep it together. "Bandit, I know you want to know what's going through my head, but I can't right now."

He held her hand a second longer and then let them slip apart. "All right."

Her chin trembled. "I'll see you tomorrow."

"Goodnight."

As she reached her room, she hurried inside and closed the door, sagging against it. She'd made Bandit talk to her without stuttering, and it didn't seem right to demand that from him and then run away, but... how could she put into words how she felt?

Robert had her feelings all over the place while they were together. Every minute was walking on eggshells. She never knew how he was going to respond. One of the conditions of accepting his marriage proposal was getting into counseling so their marriage would start off right, but there had always been a reason not to go. Why had she been so weak to allow him to push that aside?

Whatever the reason, it was a subject she'd tackle

in the morning. Her eyelids were struggling to stay open, and the bed a few feet away was calling to her.

Pushing off the door, she trudged to the bed and lay down. Tomorrow she'd apologize to Bandit without strapping him down with her emotional baggage and past failures. Another reason to keep her new husband at arm's length. He didn't need her adding to his problems.

CHAPTER 9

"What are you doing here?" asked Bear.

Bandit slid the barn door shut behind him and met his friend as he saddled his horse. "Couldn't s-s-sleep. Th-th-thought I'd help y-y-you this morning." He'd stopped by the house to drop off the second batch of cinnamon rolls and knew Bear would be getting ready to head out into the pasture.

Bear chuckled. "It's different having a woman in the house, huh?"

With a sigh, Bandit nodded. "M-m-more than I e-e-ever thought it'd b-b-be." He wouldn't tell Bear, but there'd been a crash course in that very subject the night before.

Nothing about Skye made any sense to him at all. One minute she was happily eating a cinnamon roll, and the next she was practically in tears and running from the kitchen. He couldn't figure out what went wrong. All he'd done was say he didn't want to eat one. If he'd had any smarts at all, he'd have known not to eat a sandwich before starting on the rolls.

That's why he'd been up in the first place. Well, not the sole reason. Skye was filling more and more of his thoughts. He'd be lying to himself if he said he didn't enjoy her company. Aside from the physical reason—and there were many, many things he could say about that—he liked her humor. The way she didn't mince words. She was a straight shooter, and finding a woman like that was uncommon.

All Bandit could figure was that whoever she dated in the past wasn't a good man, especially when he added in the fact that someone at some point told her she was anything less than beautiful. Other than that, he didn't have an explanation for the hot and cold she'd exhibited the night before.

"Well, get your horse saddled up, and we'll go meet Caleb. We're checking the fence today. After that last windstorm, no doubt we have some weak points."

With a nod, Bandit strode to the end of the barn to his horse, Joy. Bear and Wyatt had been taking care of her while he was away. That was another reason for joining Bear this morning. Bandit had missed his mare. By the way she behaved, like not wanting him to stop petting her and using her head to hold him to her, she'd missed him too. He promised her they'd spend more time together. It was doubtful she understood that promise, but he'd given his word, and he'd stick to it.

Once he had her ready to go, he and Bear headed out to meet Caleb, the foreman Bear hired shortly before Bandit found out about his grandfather. This would be Bandit's first time meeting him. From what Bear told Bandit, Caleb Watson was a good man and a hard worker. He took charge, kept the other ranch hands in line, and if things went wrong, he took the blame. A rare character trait as of late.

When they reached Caleb, they slowed their horses. "Hey, Caleb."

"Hey, Bear." Caleb smiled as his gaze landed on Bandit. "Hello."

"This is Bandit, my best friend," Bear said, resting his hands on the saddle horn.

"Cinnamon-roll guy?" Caleb asked as he reached a hand out to Bandit. "Those rolls of yours are famous around here."

Laughing, Bandit replied as he shook the man's hand, "That's w-w-what I'm l-l-learning. N-n-nice to meet y-y-you."

"Caleb Watson. Nice to meet you too." He looked from Bandit back to Bear. "Mark and Jayce are already headed out to the far end of the ranch. They have radios with them if anything happens. After we're done checking the fences, Mark is taking some leave to head home." Well, Bear was right about Caleb's work ethic it seemed, as he kept the small talk to a minimum.

"Everything okay? Does he need any help?" Bear asked.

Shaking his head, Caleb replied, "I got the distinct impression that I shouldn't pry, so I don't know. He did give his word that he was coming back. Up to this point, the man hasn't given me any reason to doubt him, so we'll see him sometime in January."

"All right, but if he does, you let him know I'll be happy to help." Bear took a long draw of air like it was more medicine than just a breath. "I guess we should head out."

Bandit did have to admit that when he first got back to town, he took a few deep breaths too. There was something about being in the middle of nowhere and taking in a lungful of clean air. If it affected Bear anything like it did Bandit, it made him feel energized.

"Uh, Bear..." Caleb started and stopped, pulling his

Stetson from his head and scratching the back of his neck.

"Yeah?"

"I was wanting to ask if we could hire a few more hands, especially since Mark will be leaving for the holidays." He paused and chewed the inside of his cheek. "I've got a friend who needs a job, and I think it'd be nice to maybe have a few more hands so maybe we could rotate the workload better. I mean, we have four empty cabins right now, so we *do* have a place for them."

Nodding, Bear replied, "Sounds reasonable to me. Go ahead."

"Thanks." Caleb tipped his Stetson. "I'll hit the east."

"All right. Radio if you need anything."

"Yes, sir." He set his hat back on his head and tugged on the reins, encouraging the horse to walk.

Once Caleb was out of earshot, Bear smiled. "He's a good guy. Things wouldn't run nearly as well without him."

Bandit shifted in his saddle. "S-s-seems so."

"Well, you ready to get going? When does Skye expect you back?"

Shrugging, Bandit rubbed his thumb over the saddle horn. "I d-d-did leave her a n-n-note telling her wh-wh-where I was going, but I-I-I didn't give a-a-a time." He hoped she wouldn't be upset that he left. With what happened the night before, he figured she might need a little space when she woke up. Maybe it would even give her the chance to get her thoughts put together. More than anything, he wanted her to know he was on her side.

"Then I'd say lunch. This being her second day out here, it'll be good to maybe drive her around, show her the place."

That seemed reasonable to Bandit. Long enough that she could have some space but not too long to make her think something was wrong. "I can w-w-work with th-th-that."

With the workday lined out, they urged their horses into a walk. Inspecting the fence wasn't hard, but it was tedious, and by the time they returned to the barn, his rear end reminded him just how long it had been since he'd ridden a horse.

After Joy was taken care of, Bandit slowly walked back to the cabin. Being saddle sore was embarrassing, but in his defense, even if he'd taken Joy with him to his grandfather's, he wouldn't have been able to ride her. Near the end, he was spending most of his time in a recliner in his grandpa's room, keeping watch over him in the night.

As he reached the door, he paused. It would be the first time he'd left the cabin and come back expecting someone to be there when he came home. On one hand, it was nice to know he wouldn't be alone, and on the other, it was a little nerve-wracking. Should he knock? What if she was...not properly dressed?

Instead of just barging in, he tapped his knuckles against the door and then cracked it open. "Uh, I'm back." He kept his gaze pinned to the floor as he walked in, his focus on his words.

She'd taken him by the face the night before and demanded that he not stutter when they were alone together. He'd seen the determination and sincerity in her eyes too. Taking away his place of peace upset her, and she didn't want to be responsible for it. She meant what she said about not making him uncomfortable in his own home and moving out if necessary. It was hard to form each word and then speak clearly, but it seemed her threat was the motivation he'd needed to do it. It wasn't easy to speak yet, but he'd said he'd try and meant it.

"Hope you're hungry." Her voice came from the direction of the kitchen.

"You'd be hoping right," he replied as he crossed the living room, stopping when he reached the kitchen.

Even dressed in sweatpants and a t-shirt, she wasn't any less sexy. The little bump she was sporting seemed a little bigger today too. Pregnant or not, she was attractive. Coming home to her didn't sound bad to him, especially if he could do it until he was old and gray. Which was a thought that needed to die right then and there. Being exhausted wasn't good for his brain function. As soon as he was done eating, he was taking a nap.

"Something smells good," he said as he took a few strides and sidled up next to her at the counter by the stove.

Skye laughed and pulled a pan out of the oven holding a dish with cheese melted on top. "Well, it's not my cooking. I was just keeping it warm. Gabby was coming back from dropping off some desserts, and Winnie called to ask if I wanted anything. I thought by the time you returned you'd need something to eat too."

Yawning, he covered his mouth with the back of his hand and shook his head. The long night was catching up with him quickly. He'd planned to take her on a ride like Bear suggested, but he was dragging. Add a full stomach, and there was no way he was keeping his eyes open. "Sorry."

She set the pan on the stovetop and walked to a

chair at the kitchen table, bracing her hands on the back of it. "I'm sorry about last night. I kind of went Jekyll and Hyde on you, and that wasn't right."

"That's okay." He crossed the kitchen, taking plates from the cabinet and setting them next to the stove-top. "Could you...could you tell me why?" He didn't want to pressure her, but he also didn't want to come across as not interested in why, because he was.

"Um," she said and walked to him. While she kept her gaze pinned to the plates and scooped out lasagna onto each, she said, "My ex-husband—he liked to complain about my weight and then ask me to go get treats. Much of the time, I'd order something, and he'd decide once we got there that he didn't want any."

Bandit had never been a physically violent type of man, but in that moment, he was plum positive he could pound that man into pulp. "That's not right, Skye. That's not right. I had a sandwich last night before I started making the cinnamon rolls. I made the dough first, and while it proofed, I ate. I would have never, never—" It was going to take time to get his words to come out smoothly, but he was trying, and that's all she'd wanted.

"I know." She covered one of his hands with hers. "It just hit me hard last night. I'm starting to see a lot of things about him that should've been red flags, and I just put up with it."

Laying his free hand over hers, he replied, "You never have to put up with something like that. You're worthy of more."

A small shrug. "Maybe."

He took his hand from hers, tipped her chin up, and caught her gaze. "You are, Skye." As soon as the words left his lips, he realized he'd made a mistake. It was easy to remember the kiss they'd shared at the courthouse the day prior. One he wouldn't mind sharing again.

The term *ladies' man* had never applied to him, and he hadn't dated much at all. Sure, he'd gone out on a few dates, but they'd never resulted in relationships. Mostly his fault because of his stuttering. He'd get their number and then never call. No matter how much he tried to push himself, insecurities always seemed to choke him.

Most of the time, he didn't feel he was being given permission from a woman to do more than escort her to the door and leave. But that wasn't the feeling he was getting from Skye at all. Leaning closer, her lips parted a fraction, and he could swear she even lifted on her toes a little. If that wasn't a green light, he'd call himself color-blind.

Just as he bent a little lower, his stomach growled. It may as well have been a hand slapping him across the face. She was confiding in him, and he'd nearly taken advantage of it. This wasn't the way to treat her, and he knew better.

Taking a step back, Bandit chuckled as he picked up the plates. "I guess we should have some lunch."

"Yeah, I guess so," she replied. To him, she sounded disappointed.

The more likely explanation was that it was all in his imagination. Skye didn't want more than friendship. His grumbling stomach had rescued him from messing everything up.

From now on, he'd be more careful about getting too close to her. It meant he would need to work harder at remembering the boundaries. He'd glue his head and his heart to the same page if he had to.

CHAPTER 10

He'd almost kissed her. Skye just knew it. The unfair part was that her traitorous lips tried to help him. Shoot, her whole body seemed to be in cahoots with them. What a colossal mess that would have made. Plus, it would've made things super awkward. The last thing she wanted to do was lead him on, and she was obviously not in the frame of mind to have a relationship.

Clearly her heart wasn't on the same page since the only thing she could think about was that almost kiss. And she'd wanted it. The kiss they shared the day before had come roaring back the moment his lips were close.

Then his stomach had growled. It was all she could do not to grab him by the shirt and plant one on him.

Good thing she had a few brain cells left and had the wherewithal not to act on the impetuous thought.

All through lunch, it wasn't quite awkward, but it wasn't normal between them either. Almost like he'd had the same thought she did. She knew that couldn't be true, though. Her hair was a mess, and she was dressed in sweats and a t-shirt. Not exactly the sexiest look ever.

Once they finished eating, she offered to clean up. Poor Bandit looked like he was about to fall over and took her up on the offer. Not that she was spry herself after her restless sleep, but she hadn't worked either.

Palming her forehead as she finished, she sighed as the near kiss flooded her mind again. It was like that was all she could do, obsess about something that didn't even happen. One second she was completely crushed that he hadn't kissed her, and the next, she was thanking God and anyone who was listening that it hadn't happened. It all made for a confusing situation.

She needed a nap. A long nap. One that would have her waking up with a clearer view of how to handle things. There was still a year left on this deal, and she was already wrestling with herself.

With a soft groan, she used a little momentum to

push off the counter and cross the kitchen into the living room.

The television was on, but Bandit was out. And not in the most comfortable position either. He'd taken an end seat on the couch, set his feet on the coffee table, and his head wasn't quite touching his left shoulder. If he stayed that way, his neck would hurt for days. He must be tired to stay in a position that had to be uncomfortable.

She walked to him and bent down. "Bandit, you should go lie down."

Glazed-over eyes met hers as he lifted his head. "Okay," he whispered. His eyes slid shut, and his chin dropped to his chest before the word was fully out of his mouth.

"Hey, you. Come on." She gently shook him.

When he didn't respond, she tried to think of something else. "I guess lying on the couch is better than nothing." She took his face in her hands. "Bandit, scoot over a little."

He didn't even look at her. He just shifted on the couch a little more each time she encouraged him to move a little more. Eventually, she managed to get him stretched out on the couch. After, she went in search of a blanket and then covered him with it before sitting on the edge of the couch a moment.

Good-looking was a lackluster word for Bandit Ochoa. Even hot didn't quite describe him anymore. His heart and kindness took him to a level most men wouldn't hit even if they stood on their tiptoes. He'd woken up in the middle of the night to eat, and then he'd made her cinnamon rolls. She'd lost the bet, yet he'd still done it because he knew she wanted them.

It was sweet and thoughtful and everything Robert wasn't. If she were still married, she'd probably be the one getting up in the middle of the night to take care of him—selfish loser. What did that make her for putting up with him? A loser times two?

Covering Bandit's hand with hers, she gave a soft squeeze and went to stand.

His fingers gripped hers, holding her still. "You can lie down with me." It came out like mumble soup, but she was fluent in that language, having grown up with a brother who she took care of while their parents worked.

Bandit was cute, but... "There's not enough room for both of us." Her mouth took off before she'd had the chance to think about an answer.

She rolled her eyes. Why did she say that? She didn't need to be lying down with him. One more close encounter like the one earlier, and her stupid hormonal lips might just pucker up despite the sane reasoning that said she shouldn't. "I mean…"

Rolling to his side, he faced her and plastered himself to the back of the couch. "Plenty of…" The sentence trailed off as he lifted the covers for her. "Or I can give you the couch."

"No, no. That's okay." She blew out a puff of air, frustrated with herself. "I'll just go…"

When he lifted his half-open eyes to hers, a faint smile on his lips, he looked better than any man she'd ever seen. "The TV on helps me sleep. It might help you."

Her head bobbed up and down like it was perched on a spring. "Okay."

She situated herself with her back against him and let out a deep breath. Actually, it felt great because she'd sort of propped herself against Bandit. Not exactly on her side, but not flat either. Of course, her belly was peeking over the edge of the couch, but not too badly. She hadn't realized how deep the couch was. That was a bit of a nice surprise.

By the time she was settled, Bandit was sound asleep again with his arm hanging across her stomach. All those times she'd read about people fitting together had sounded ridiculous. Now that she was experiencing it, it wasn't silly at all. The way he curved around her gave her comfort. It made her feel like she belonged right where she was. Something she hadn't ever felt before, and especially not with Robert.

When she'd agreed to this arrangement, she'd made a deal with herself that she'd end the year having a better understanding of herself and what she wanted. This was going to the top of her list. If she didn't fit physically with a man, then she wouldn't fit mentally or emotionally.

That's if she fit with someone again. Did you get two chances, or was that a once-in-a-lifetime thing? She held in a groan. Why was she even thinking about that? Bandit was a good man. She liked him, but this deal of theirs wasn't the way to start a relationship.

Aside from that, he was too nice. This baby wasn't his, and he was the kind of man to step up even when that wasn't what he wanted. No way would she put him in that sort of position. Not when he'd already been so wonderful.

No, she'd be grateful and appreciative. Then she'd go her merry way, despite the little pinch it gave her heart. It was the best thing for both of them.

CHAPTER 11

The pressure Bandit felt on his chest was confusing as he slowly woke up. It wasn't unpleasant, just different. The more he gathered his wits, the quicker he realized where the heaviness was coming from: Skye.

A fuzzy memory played of a conversation between them, but at the time, he thought it was a dream. He wouldn't complain, though. Now that he was wide awake, he didn't mind it at all.

If there ever was a woman who fit against him, it was her. There wasn't an empty space anywhere on him. To him, it seemed as though she'd been made just for him. Even more than the way she fit, he liked how her hair was draped over his neck, the way her head rested against his arm like a pillow, and waking with her next to him. Eighty years or so of that would be just fine with him.

All in all, there wasn't a negative thing he could come up with. He knew this marriage deal would come to an end in a year, but part of him had to wonder if he could show her that staying wouldn't be so bad.

He could take care of her and the baby. Who cared if the baby was his or not? If Bandit claimed the little bundle of blessing, then wouldn't that make the baby his? He certainly wanted kids, and his momma always said that you didn't argue with God on how He delivered things that were prayed for. He knew she'd say Bandit should give thanks and appreciate that God heard the plea and loved him enough to answer.

Skye took a deep breath and shifted onto her back. A moment later, her eyes flew open, and she was staring up at Bandit. "I'm so sorry."

Before she could move, he stilled her. "Sorry for what?"

"I'm taking up the whole couch with my big butt."

"I'm not complaining, am I? And you don't have a big butt." His eyes widened as he realized what flew out of his mouth. "Not that I've been…looking at your butt. Or that your butt shouldn't be looked at…" Oh, dear Lord. He squeezed his eyes shut. "I'm so sorry."

A second later, Skye sneezed, and Bandit opened his eyes.

Her smile stretched from one ear to the next. She wasn't sneezing, she was trying to hold in a giggle.

"That's not nice," he said.

Another giggle popped out. "I've never heard you talk so fast."

He grunted. "Me either."

They both burst out laughing, and he loved it. It was genuine, just like her. Slowly, it tapered off, and Skye sighed. "I'm sorry for taking more than my share of the couch."

"You didn't," he said as their gazes locked.

Bear once told him that when he shared a look with Winnie, the world would fall away. At the time, Bandit didn't have a frame of reference for that. Now, he understood with complete clarity what his friend was talking about. A dome lowering over him, cutting out all the clutter and chaos of the world and leaving him alone with a woman he was falling for.

Bandit's heart thundered in his ears as the words trotted across his mind. It was pointless to deny it. There wasn't an argument made that could shift what he knew to be true. Who wouldn't fall for her? Well, her idiot ex, but stupid men were a dime a dozen. It was the smart ones who found a good woman and held on to them.

He also knew she'd been hurt by that idiot of a man. She'd need more than words to convince her that Bandit wouldn't behave like that. Skye would need actions and deeds. Things that proved he'd be faithful and loving and a good father. Someone she could depend on to stick around when things were tough. He could do that too.

Suddenly, it hit him that maybe he was getting ahead of himself. Just because he thought she might have been giving him permission to kiss her earlier didn't mean she was. There was a high likelihood that he'd seen what he wanted because he was now keenly aware that he wanted her—all of her.

Before he could delve too deep into the thought, he said, "I thought maybe I could drive you around the ranch. Show it to you. There's a good spot for watching the sunset. We could pack a picnic if you want."

Nodding, she smiled. "I'd really like that."

"We could even stay and look at the stars. Without all the light pollution, they're endless."

"It's been a long time since I've done that." She looked down. "My parents took us camping a few times, and I didn't appreciate it then. I was young and wanted to talk with my friends."

"I'd offer to camp, but I don't think the ground would be all that comfortable for you."

She shook her head and chuckled. "No, it seems I've waved comfort goodbye until I have the baby."

He tilted his head. "Is your bed okay?"

"It's fine. My back and hips ache, but this little munchkin loves kickboxing my organs." She rubbed her hand over her stomach and grimaced. "Oh, there he goes—not that I know it's a he."

"I guess I didn't realize when you'd start feeling the baby move." Carrie Anne had let him feel her baby kick, and Bandit had thought it was the most amazing thing. It was one thing to know life was growing; it was another to feel it.

Skye took Bandit's hand and set it on her stomach. "See?" she asked.

Either the baby's hand or foot connected with his hand. "Little one has a serious right hook, huh?"

"So it's not just me?" She snorted. "I feel like I'm carrying the Hulk."

Another hard kick, and Bandit looked at her. "It's not just you. Man, he's feisty." It also meant the little fighter was making it hard on his momma when it came to sleeping. He leaned in closer to her tummy. "Hey, you, be nice."

This time when the baby moved, it felt more like a push. "Maybe he'll be reasonable once he gets here," he said with a laugh and glanced up at Skye.

"Or maybe he just like your voice." The way she said it, there was no teasing or joking lacing the words.

"Naw." He cleared his throat. If he didn't move, he'd kiss her. A move they might both regret. He might have feelings for her, but that didn't mean she returned them. She was a nice person. "I guess I'll get up, get a shower, and then put us a picnic together. I'll meet you at the door in, say, an hour?"

"Make it two and you're on. I want to soak in that tub you put in." She grinned and moved so he could stand.

"Yes, ma'am. Two it is." As he stood, he helped her up, planting a kiss on her forehead. Embarrassment flooded him, and his feet couldn't move fast enough. "I'll s-s-see you." He threw the statement over his shoulder as he bolted from the room.

He needed to get himself together. Even if there was a chance he could prove to her he wasn't like her ex, it didn't mean she'd want Bandit. Sure, he was talking better, but that wasn't the sum of a relationship. There were other factors to consider. What if she didn't want to live on the ranch? She did have a florist shop in Amarillo. It was a successful business. She wouldn't want to leave that for him.

Of course, he could leave the ranch for Amarillo, but just the idea of living in the city made his pulse quicken. It was too big for him. He liked the slow pace of life and the small town. Ever since he'd moved to Caprock Canyon with his mom, he'd pictured raising his own kids here.

He huffed as he shut his bedroom door. Why was he thinking about that stuff? They had a contract. He'd respect her and the terms. It wasn't right to do any less. From this point on, he'd do his best to keep that at the forefront of his mind, no matter what his heart had to say about the matter. He'd be her friend, and that was good enough.

"GLAD BEAR GRADED THIS ROAD." Bandit glanced at Skye sitting in the passenger seat of his truck. "Otherwise, we'd be busting our heads open."

She chuckled. "Bad, huh?"

He nodded. "The first time he brought me out here, he was celebrating just purchasing the place.

This road was rough. Even going slower than slow, it was awful."

"You said Bear bought the place?"

"Yeah. He'd wanted it for as long as I knew him, so when he won that lottery, it was one of the first purchases he made. I'd never been so happy for someone. He'd dreamed of fixing the place up. Ever since he got the house renovated, his family has spent Thanksgiving through Christmas here."

"Did you stay at the house?"

"Nah," he replied and quickly added, "Not that they didn't offer. They did. Mrs. West nearly threatened to chain me to a room, but I like my cabin. It's comfortable. Plus, as much as I feel like family, I know they need their time together."

"The holidays at my parents' house is always a mixed bag." Skye crossed her arms over her chest. "Most of the time, I'm torn. On one hand, I love them and I want to spend time with them. On the other, I know at some point they're going to make an off-hand remark and hurt my feelings."

That didn't sit well with Bandit. "They don't know how it makes you feel?"

"It's mostly my mom. She's into makeup and fashion and looking nice at all times. She's found a new diet almost every time I talk to her. I just, for me, life is about being happy. None of that stuff makes me happy." She snorted. "I love cake and flowers and being comfortable. I don't like all that heavy makeup on my face."

"You definitely don't need makeup. You wake up picture-ready." She'd changed from the sweatpants and t-shirt to leggings and a light-pink flowy shirt that hung loose. The color was such a contrast with her dark hair and eyes. She was stunning.

She gently popped him on the arm. "That's not true."

He glanced at her. "It is too. I was there."

"Oh, hush." She tried to hide a smile, but she couldn't quite keep it off her lips. "You…flatterer."

"I am not. I tell how I see it. You're pretty all the time." He winked.

She exhaled as she shook her head. "Now I know you're full of it."

Bandit couldn't understand the people who had created such doubt in Skye. Her mom. Her rat of an ex-husband. The folks she was supposed to be able to count on to lift her up. He'd never understand that sort of thing.

The first person who floated to mind was his own father. It was so easy to wonder why others reacted the way they did. How they let things control them, but when he turned that microscope on himself, he was no less guilty.

How long had Bandit allowed his dad's words to live in his head. That he was dumb. That he'd never amount to anything. All sorts of things dads aren't supposed to say to their kids. Bandit had taken all those words in, let them settle into his heart and live in him. It was certainly something to ponder and work on. But another day. Now, it was time to sit outside, eat dinner with a beautiful woman, and enjoy the sunset.

"You hungry?" he asked.

"Starved." She smiled and pushed open the door, taking a deep breath. "I like it out here. The air is crisp."

Stepping out of the truck, Bandit shut the door and opened the back so he could grab the basket. "One of the reasons I love living out here. It's quiet and gives a person time to just be." He shut the back door, walked around the back of the pickup, and met Skye just as she started to step down.

"I've never been so thankful for running boards," she said as she held on to the door for balance.

"I'm sorry about that." He rubbed the back of his neck. "It can get pretty deep with snow out here. I didn't want to get stuck when you go into labor."

Skye lifted her gaze to his. "Wait. You didn't have this truck before we made our agreement?"

He grimaced. "No?"

"Bandit, you've done all these nice things for me. I would've been fine." She stepped onto the ground and palmed his chest. "But thank you. I'm very appreciative."

Covering her hand with his, he said, "I know. That's part of why I did it. I like seeing you smile." The second it left his lips, he froze. He didn't want things to be weird between them. Nor did he want to ruin the evening.

Her cheeks bloomed pink. "Uh, let's get that blanket spread out, okay?"

"You bet," he said, backing up so she could get to the back passenger door.

As soon as she turned around, he rolled his eyes. He needed to watch what he said. It had only been two days, and he was already on the verge of messing up their friendship. He'd just have to go back to keeping his mouth shut as much as possible. That seemed to be the only way to fix things, even if it made his heart pout. It would just have to get over it.

CHAPTER 12

With her legs stretched out in front of her, Skye leaned back on her elbows. Bandit had packed sandwiches and brought a couple of cinnamon rolls along. It had been perfect, and now the sun was slowly descending into the horizon, painting the sky russet-orange, purple, and yellow as far as the eye could see. "This is nice."

"Yeah, it is. Quiet and peaceful." He was lying next to her on the blanket with his hands beneath his head. "It's funny. It always seems that the sunset is quick, but out here, it's almost like it knows it's being watched and it slows down so a person can enjoy it."

"It does seem that way." She smiled and glanced at Bandit. His words were jerky, but she could tell he was trying. She truly didn't care about him stuttering. Home was his refuge, and she didn't want to take that away from him.

Waking up next to him had sent her nervous system into overload. The way he was looking at her when she woke up, with a smile on his lips and in his eyes, seemed like he was happy to see her. If she was honest with herself, she'd say the same thing about him. A gorgeous man looking at her with longing and desire? What woman wouldn't want to wake up to a man like that?

He'd been so cute when he got flustered talking about her butt. His mouth had hit fourth gear and the nitro button at the same time. The blush on his cheeks. How he'd squeezed his eyes shut in frustration. She'd tried to hold back a laugh and couldn't.

Then he'd held her gaze, shutting out the world. Never had she ever wanted to be kissed by a man more than in that moment. She'd forgotten all her reasons for not being with him, but just as quickly, they'd returned when the baby kicked her pancreas.

Taking his hand, she'd placed it on her tummy. The smile he'd given her, the wonderment in his eyes. It felt like not only was she where she was supposed to be, but the baby was too. That maybe he wouldn't feel imposed on to take that role. Bandit would be the best father Skye and the baby could have.

When she first found out she was pregnant, one of the things that made her heart ache was the thought of going through everything alone. Doctor's appointments, picking out furniture, taking pictures when they were trying to decipher instructions and put toys together. Naming their child. She'd wanted to share feeling the baby move with her husband…and she had with Bandit as her husband, but it just didn't feel the same. There was a time limit that tinged the moment with sadness. The other side of that was, would Robert even have cared? As much as it hurt to think about, her answer came in a resounding, *No*.

Bandit cared, though. There was no mistaking it with the goofy grin on his face. His voice was full of excitement. Then the way he talked to the baby… She'd choked back tears. It was so sweet. She wasn't kidding about his voice either. Skye loved his voice. It was deep and smooth. Now that he wasn't stuttering, it was easier to hear just what a great voice he had.

She sat up and rubbed her elbows. Sitting like that was okay for a while, but now her arms hurt. A small groan came from her as she tried to work out the aches. Maybe it was a good thing. She didn't need to be thinking all this stuff about Bandit.

"You okay?"

"I'm fine, but I should've known better than to sit like that." Now her back was hurting too, along with her hips.

Bandit rolled to his side and propped himself up on his elbow. "You can lean on me. I don't mind if it'll help you. Or we can go back home. I'm okay either way."

She shook her head. "I don't want to squeeze the juice out of you, and I really don't want to go home. I'd like to see the stars."

He chuckled. "My momma used to say that…'squeeze the juice.' I always laughed when she said it. You're not gonna hurt me if you want to use me as a prop. All I care about is you being comfortable."

"That's a kind offer. I think I just need to get used to the fact that things I normally do aren't happening until I have this little tummy nugget." She used her right hand to rub her left shoulder. "From here, it'll only get worse."

Bandit sat up and scooted until he was behind her. He set his hands on her shoulders, gently kneading them. "Is this okay?"

Okay? "Actually, it's great. A little harder maybe?"

With that, he went to work, and all she could do was moan every time he worked a knot out of her muscles. It had been forever since she'd been to a massage therapist, and it felt wonderful. Enough so that if she were facedown on a masseuse table, she'd be asleep by now.

The massage slowly came to an end, and she sighed, turning to him slightly. "Thank you."

He rubbed his hands together. "Give me a bit of time and I can do more. My hands were cramping a little."

"No, that's okay. This was amazing. I feel so much better." She smiled.

He motioned with his hands to her. "Come on. Lean back on me. We'll look at the stars and then go home."

For a second, she hesitated and then situated herself until her back was flush against him. "You're so good to me."

"It's not all that hard." The vibration of his laugher rolled through her.

Not all that hard. Maybe for Bandit, but she couldn't say the same about her ex. Why was she just now realizing how selfish the man was? Maybe she'd known it all along and now that she was experiencing something better, someone better, it made it all the more a stark contrast.

As she considered all the things going on in her mind, she laid her head back on Bandit's shoulder and watched stars slowly fill up the sky as it turned black. "It's so easy to forget how limitless the sky is when you're in the city all the time."

"My first night back at the cabin, I felt the same way." He paused, inhaling deeply. "I don't think I could ever tire of being out here."

"I wonder how many people could use something like this." She crossed her arms over her chest. "Being able to stay somewhere like this so they could reset and recharge."

His hands came to rest on her arms. "Somewhere in the middle of nowhere. A place that forced people to disconnect from electronics and connect with people?"

Skye quickly craned her neck to look at Bandit. Silly move, really, since it was so black. The only reason she knew he was there was that she could feel him against her. "Yeah, a place like that. You could advertise it to people who feel like their life is out of control. Somewhere they could hide to figure out what they want to do without distraction. A place where they could reflect."

"I've actually thought about that too. I love the Wests, love cooking for them at the holidays, but they don't need me anymore. They've got Winnie and Reagan. Not that they've made me feel that way, but I want something I can call mine."

"I understand that. It's one of the reasons I started my flower shop. That, and I love flowers." She turned to face Bandit with her legs hooked over one of his. "Anything and all things flowers. Have you thought a lot about opening something like that?"

"Not a whole lot. Just here and there. Most of what stopped me was the idea of being alone."

"That makes sense. If you could open up a place like that, would you stay in Texas?"

Chuckling, he said, "Funny you should ask that. I've caught myself on land websites looking at South Dakota or Wyoming. I'd like somewhere near the mountains."

"I love the mountains too." She smiled. "When I was a kid, one of our vacations was to see Mount Rushmore. I loved looking out the hotel room and seeing the mountains stretching the entire horizon."

"I was poor growing up. Momma worked hard, and she made enough. She just didn't have it to splurge on vacations. Plus, we didn't have anyone to run the restaurant if she did go anywhere."

During their talks before they got married, he'd told her a little about his childhood. "I bet that was hard."

"Not really. I had no idea we were poor. I never went hungry, and we had a roof over our heads. When I was old enough to work, I helped with paying the bills. I wouldn't exactly say we were comfortable, but we didn't hurt too bad. We just couldn't afford fancy things."

Part of her was sad to hear that. "I'm sorry."

"Why? I had a momma who loved me. What she lacked in money, she more than made up for in other ways. As a little boy, I hardly went a night without her reading to me. When I was older, she'd make sure to sit down with me at the restaurant when I got out of school. Didn't matter how busy the place was, she'd give me no less than an hour of her time. Then at night, she'd check every piece of my homework." His voice broke, and he paused. "I didn't have money, but I wouldn't trade what I did have for all the gold in Fort Knox."

Wrapping her arms around his neck, Skye held him to her. She wanted to say something, but words seemed to fail her. What was there to say? She'd already told him he was sweet. That he was kind and thoughtful. Generous. "Your momma would be so proud of the man you've become."

His arms circled around her. "Thank you."

The longer they held each other, the more she didn't want to let go or be let go of. She knew Bandit was a different man than Robert. Really, there was no comparison at all anymore.

She had a life to return to, though. Her cousin was going to run the flower shop while Skye spent the year with Bandit. She hadn't given her business away. Plus, she didn't need to be going from one relationship to the next. She needed time to work on herself. To figure out who she was and what she wanted. How could she offer anything to Bandit when she was struggling to love herself?

Pregnancy hormones didn't help either. Did she really even know what she was feeling right now? The answer that came to mind the quickest was *no*. There was a real chance that everything she felt was simply amplified by them. Did she want to give birth and a few months later realize that while she liked Bandit, she didn't love him? It would be wrong to do that to Bandit, especially after all the kind things he'd done for her.

Then there was the issue of commitment. She

wasn't ready for that. With the baby coming, her life was going to change in so many ways, and while it would be nice to have a man by her side, she didn't want to think that was the only way she'd make it work. She could be a strong single mother. Just like Bandit's mom.

Slowly, the hug ended and Bandit pulled away. As he did, his cheek brushed against hers, and for a split second, his lips lingered near hers before putting distance between them. "I guess we should get back to the house," he said, his voice thick. "That nap's wearing off."

Was it wrong to feel disappointed he didn't kiss her? Even after listing all the reasons she had for not staying with him, there she was, wanting what she shouldn't be wanting. Leading him on would be wrong, and she knew it. "Yeah, mine is too." A total and complete lie. She was wide awake now. That tiny moment of anticipation had her heart fluttering in her chest.

It was for the best, though. Bandit didn't need an indecisive pregnant woman messing up his life and hurting him. Until Skye was solidly on her own two feet and thinking clearly, even considering a relationship—with Bandit or anyone else—was foolish.

She needed time to process her relationship with

Robert and figure out where she wanted to be in life and how she was going to handle her future. At least, that's what her head was saying. Her heart had other ideas, ones she'd not entertain at the moment. It would just have to sit and sulk.

CHAPTER 13

In the two weeks following Bandit's picnic with Skye, the night had played in his head almost constantly. Mostly because he and Skye were more like roommates now. He'd been so close to kissing her that night, and the next day, it felt like a wall had slammed down between them.

It was just as well. He knew the relationship wasn't real, and if they'd spent more time together, it would've just made his mixed-up feelings worse. That near kiss was probably the reason for the not-quite-silent treatment. If he'd just kept a handle on how much he liked her.

He wouldn't describe his feelings as love at first sight, but there'd been a bushel of like. Those feelings had taken root, though, and the strangers-passing-in-the-hall vibe hadn't lessened them in the least. Normally, Bandit would be heading out to work with Bear, but he wasn't working today. It was Saturday, and Wyatt and Gabby were having a larger than normal farmer's market. With Thursday being Thanksgiving, it was the perfect time for people to get goodies for their office parties or order them so they'd be ready for their feast on Thursday.

Of course, he'd already taken Skye to the orchard, but it hadn't felt right. She'd stuck to Winnie during the visit, which left Bandit on his own. Since Bear knew the relationship wasn't real, he thought nothing of it and stayed with Winnie.

All Bandit could envision for the day was a repeat of last time. In truth, he was almost dreading it, but he'd take Skye so she could have fun. As if he had a choice. Winnie had made him promise. Well, he wasn't the only one. Almost like she knew what Skye would do, Winnie made her promise too and then upped the ante with the promise of crème brûlée. If Skye wanted it, she'd have to attend.

The grumbling and ranting after Winnie left was funny. He'd never heard so many *wretched redhead* and *she'll get hers one day* statements. Boy, Skye was so hot, Bandit almost expected her hair to turn fiery red.

"Okay. I'm ready."

He looked up from the recliner he was occupying, and his breath caught. How did she get prettier every time he saw her? Standing, he smiled. "That dress really is pretty on you." The soft yellow with her brown sweater was perfect on her. At least she was wearing leggings to keep her legs warm.

Waving him off, she ducked her head, but not before he saw a pink blush blanket her cheeks. "I've outgrown all my jeans. One second I could wear them, and the next, I couldn't shimmy them past my calves. Doesn't help that this belly is in the way."

"Your belly is fine. A person is growing in there."

Skye held her hands out, waved them down her body, and sighed. "I look terrible. I'm fat in all the wrong places, my thighs rub together so badly I could start forest fires, and I can't see my feet!"

Bandit was on the move before his brain could protest. Wrapping his arms around her, he said, "You are a beautiful pregnant woman. Your body is going through changes, and I won't begin to know how hard that is." He leaned back and was met with tear-filled eyes. "Your positives far outweigh any negatives you could think of."

"And now I'm whiney." Her chin trembled.

One way or another, she'd have a smile on before they left. "And cute."

Another sniff. "I haven't shaved my legs in a month."

"Me either."

Her lips rolled in, and she choked a laugh. "That wasn't funny."

He took one of his hands and pointed his finger at her lips. "Do they know that?"

Grabbing his finger, she was trying her best to give him the hardest look she had. "Yes."

"I don't think so." He smiled. "Now, stop being stubborn and show me that smile. You know which one I'm talking about too."

Skye tilted her head. "What smile?"

He chuckled. "The one that makes your whole face light up. It's got to be the best smile I've ever seen."

"You haven't looked in a mirror recently, have you?" She grinned, and her eyebrows rose together. "See, I can play that blush game too."

Man, he'd missed this. It had only been a couple of weeks, but the absence of her laughter and humor was profound. "Can we be friends again?"

Her mouth parted slightly. "I'm so sorry you felt that way. It really wasn't you. It was me."

"I promise not to do anything that'll make you uncomfort—"

The sentence died as her lips touched his. She

leaned back, her eyes wide. Like she hadn't planned it at all. "I just wanted to see if..." She didn't finish before touching her lips to his again.

What was he supposed to do? He knew what he wanted to do, but should he? His lips sure thought so, because they weren't listening to his rational side. The one that said this was probably a huge mistake. Instead, he matched her light kisses until there was nothing left but need.

He circled his arms around her a little tighter, sliding his hand up her back and into her hair as her arms locked around his neck. He loved the feel of her body against his. Once the baby was here, she'd fit just as perfect facing him as she had with her back to him on the couch.

His lips moved in rhythm with hers, and as her lips parted, he deepened the kiss. The feverish way she kissed him set his blood on fire. He'd never kissed like this before. Like a woman was feeling the same desire for him as he was for her. The desperate kisses continued long enough that he was struggling to catch his breath.

When his lungs screamed, he broke the kiss and set his forehead against hers. His heart hammered against his ribs, and his chest heaved as he sucked in lungsful of air. The best part was that it seemed Skye was as breathless as him.

They stood there, tangled together, holding each other as if one of them might get away. "Skye..." he said.

"Please, don't say anything." She pulled back and met his gaze. "I don't want to hurt you. I swear I don't."

What he could see in her eyes was so much confusion. He knew she'd enjoyed the kiss. You didn't kiss someone with that sort of passion and not like it. She was pregnant, still dealing with a bad relationship, and she was a sweetheart of a woman who wouldn't want to hurt a fly.

"You're pregnant. I'm sorry too."

Her lips pursed together, and she continued to hold his gaze as if there was a full-on war being waged. "It's my fault. I'm...it was wrong of me to do that. I guess I'm feeling a little lonely."

"I know that feeling well." He did, too. So well. Surrounded by people he knew loved him, and yet, he may as well have been on Mars for how utterly alone he felt. "It's okay."

Skye's shoulders sagged. "No, it wasn't. I didn't want to make things weird, and now I have."

Bandit forced a smile. "No, ma'am. We're right as rain." A monsoon was going so strong in his heart that he was surprised a small dark cloud hadn't appeared over his head. He wouldn't say anything to hurt her, though, and he wouldn't hold it against her either. Not when her emotions were in such a state of confusion.

If there was one thing that stuck with him, it was that he wasn't ever going to be like his daddy and leave when things were hard. It would be hard to be around her knowing he was falling for her, but he could do it. He'd faced harder things than this. At least she cared enough to think of him and not want to hurt him.

"Are you ready to go?" he asked.

"Yeah," she replied softly.

Bandit stepped aside and then followed her to the door where he helped her get her coat on.

Turning to face him, she palmed his chest. "I don't know what's wrong with me. I seem to have a knack for messing things up. I'm so sorry. I'm just..." Her gaze dropped to the floor.

Covering her hand with his, he tipped her chin up with a finger on his free hand. "You haven't messed anything up. Nothing. I caught Carrie Anne eating a marshmallow-and-mayonnaise sandwich one time. I still get queasy thinking about it. I'll take an errant kiss over that any day."

"Ew." She startled. "Not the kiss, the sandwich. If

you see something like that in my hand, take it from me. That's just gross."

Laughing, Bandit took his hand from hers and grabbed his coat and hat. "I'm not taking anything from a pregnant woman."

She shrugged. "Yeah, you're probably right."

He held the door for her, following her out before shutting it behind him. His plan now was to make this day great for her. Yeah, he was mighty disappointed about her reaction to the kiss. It would be one that all others would never eclipse. That thought hurt a little, but he'd survive.

Though, this did pose a challenge. They had eleven and a half more months together. His heart already felt a little shredded on the edges. Boy, he sure wished his grandpa was still around. He'd know what to do. Anything would be better than picking up a broken heart this time next year.

CHAPTER 14

If she could, Skye would crawl under a rock and never come out again. She'd kissed Bandit. Kissed him with all she had and enjoyed every single minute of it. Then he'd spoken her name, and her fight-or-flight engaged. She'd ruined the entire moment.

It was the best kiss of her life. That man's mouth might have been horrible for talking, but, have mercy, he was a masterful kisser. If she could've, she'd have told Winnie to kick rocks and stayed home kissing him. It was a whole lot better than Winnie's deserts.

Bandit's truck came to a stop, and he cut the engine. "Time for some fun."

"Yep," she said, grabbing the handle and stepping out of the truck faster than Bandit could race around to help her.

He set his hands on his hips as he reached her. "Now why'd you do that? I don't mind helping you."

"I wanted to see if I could do it." Liar, liar, pants en fuego. She didn't want to get that close to him again. She was changing her mind so much her neck was aching from the whiplash. Back and forth and back and forth. She was swinging so hard and fast it was a wonder she could hang on.

"Okay. Just…we're good. I promise." He added a half-grin and winked.

This man.

"Bandit!"

Skye knew who that voice belonged to. Bear.

Bandit walked a few paces and shook Bear's hand.

Not only could Bandit kiss like a pro, but he had a butt on him too. "Hey, Bear," Skye said, shaking her head and hoping no one saw the wanton ogling she'd given Bandit's behind.

Winnie joined Bear, hugging his bicep with her arms. "Hi, Bandit." Then her gaze fell on Skye.

Crud. That woman could catch a fly Mr. Miyagi style. Winnie winked as if she knew what Skye was thinking. "You got that crème brûlée?" Skye asked.

"Yep, and some *butt*ermilk pie too." She grinned.

Bandit looked from Skye to Winnie. "Is th-th-there something I'm m-m-missing?"

Skye vigorously shook her head and latched onto Winnie's arm, pulling her from Bear. "Why don't we go over there somewhere and talk about them," Skye said.

Once Skye was sure they were in the clear, she turned on Winnie. "You are a troublemaker."

"I wasn't the one staring at Bandit's butt in public."

"I—" Skye took a deep breath, and her cheeks puffed out before releasing it. "Hush. It's his fault anyway. If he didn't have such a great behind, I wouldn't be looking at it."

Carrie Anne sidled up to Winnie with her daughter, Camry, in her arms. "Behind? What behind?"

"Nothing!" Skye blurted as Winnie said, "Bandit's butt."

"Oh?" Carrie Anne perked up.

From what Skye was told, this woman was the matchmaker of Caprock Canyon. Meddlesome, crafty, and hard-headed. "Oh, no." Skye shook her head. "Nope. No way."

Winnie laughed. "Oh, she's got it bad."

"I have nothing bad except…." Well, she couldn't say choice in men because that would lump Bandit in there, and he was far superior to any man she'd ever run across. "I'm pregnant. Carrie Anne, you should know that hormones are whack right now."

Winnie's grin widened. "I know all about it." Skye knew they'd been trying.

Carrie Anne gulped air and hugged her. "And you didn't wait until Christmas?"

She giggled. "No, because everyone expects it now. I haven't told King or Caroline yet, but I'm planning to sneak it on them somehow."

Skye wrapped her in a hug too. "I'm so happy for you." She'd known Bear and Winnie were trying.

"I was feeling so sick to my stomach about a week before. Bear suggested I take one, and there it was..." She touched her stomach. "I only found out a couple of weeks ago. I think I was a little scared to tell anyone."

Camry began to get restless, and Carrie Anne swayed back and forth. "I'm thrilled."

Winnie looked at Skye. "Now, back to Bandit."

Skye rolled her eyes. "He's nice and kind. But this marriage is only temporary. I don't even know how I'm feeling. I didn't mean to k—" She stopped short. Her mouth. Just once could it have some sort of connection with her brain? "Karate-chop him."

Winnie pinched the bridge of her nose. "Oh my word, girl." She lifted her gaze to Skye's. "You kissed him?"

Looking from Winnie to Carrie Ann and back, she replied, "I said I karate-chopped him."

"We've been to the gym together. You can't touch your toes any better than I can, especially now." Winnie shook her head. "Now, about that k—"

Skye shushed her. "I'm not talking about this. Especially in front of Mrs. Matchmaker."

Carrie Anne feigned offense. "Me? I can't help if I'm right all the time."

"Neither of you is right about this," she scolded, pointing one finger at Carrie Anne and then at Winnie. "I'm pregnant. My hormones are on overload. This is not the time to be thinking about a relationship."

Rolling her lips in, Winnie rocked on her feet. "We weren't talking about a relationship. We were talking about a kiss. Is there something else we should be discussing?"

Skye rubbed her face with her hands. Was she in high school or something? Sheesh. She dropped her hands to her side. "No. Nothing needs to be discussed."

Winnie held her hands up. "Okay. Fine. You're right. We'll keep our noses out of it."

Nodding, Carrie Anne said, "Scouts honor."

"Good." Skye set her hands on her hips. "No funny business." The sound of footsteps came from behind her, and she redirected the conversation. "Now, about that crème brûlée."

Winnie rolled her eyes. "You'll have it before you leave. No worries."

Bandit smiled. "Congratulations, Winnie."

Skye nearly jumped hearing his voice. She turned and plastered on a smile to hide her surprise. "Isn't it great?"

Winnie's cheeks lifted so high her eyes were half-moons. "Thank you."

Taking Winnie in his arms, Bear hugged her to him. "I never thought I'd have this." He looked at Carrie Anne. "If you hadn't been so all-fired nosey, Winnie might not be here. I don't know that I've ever said thank you."

Skye stood there, listening to the exchange. How had she been so lucky to fall into the path of this family? If it weren't for Winnie, there was no telling where Skye would be.

Carrie Anne smiled. "I'm just glad you found her."

If Skye didn't get out of there, she'd dissolve into a puddle of tears. What was happening to her? All this sentimental stuff. She hated feeling like all she could do was cry. She rubbed her stomach and silently scolded herself and the baby. They needed to keep it together.

Almost as if Bandit could hear her thoughts, he put his arm around her waist and leaned in to whisper, "You w-w-want to go walk a-a-around?"

"Yes." Skye waved bye to Winnie, Bear, Carrie Anne, and Camry. "I'll catch up with you later."

They waved back, and as soon as they were out of earshot, Skye heaved a sigh of relief. "Thank you for the save back there. My sappy meter was at max capacity."

"Th-th-they are little s-s-sugary, huh?" Bandit chuckled.

"So, it's not just me?"

Shaking his head, he said, "No. I usually see my way out too."

Her phone chimed in her pocket, and she pulled it out. "It's my mom. Probably to double-check that we're coming for Thanksgiving."

"Okay."

She put the phone to her ear. "Hey, Mom."

"She answers," her mom chided.

Rolling her eyes, Skye looked at Bandit. "I answer my phone all the time."

"One out of six calls is not all the time." Her mom huffed. "I was just calling to make sure you're still planning to come for Thanksgiving on Thursday."

"Yep. Still planning on it."

Her mom paused, and Skye could see the look on her face like she was standing right in front of her. The scowl. "Skye, please dress nicely. I know it's just a family dinner, but you should take care of yourself, especially now that you're having a baby."

"I will." If for no other reason than to keep her mom from pouncing on her the moment she walked into her parents' house. "I'll see you Thursday, okay?"

"Okay, sweetheart." She paused and then added, "Bandit's coming as well, right?"

Skye looked at Bandit. "He is. You're really going to like him." Then it hit her, and internally she withered. He was most likely going to stutter while they were there. Her mom would latch on to the one thing he struggled with, and that would be all she'd see.

"Well, good. We'll see you then."

They said their goodbyes, and Skye sagged. "I have to find something that will fit me and keep my mom off my back."

Bandit nodded. "All right. I think Gabby said something about a little shop here. They started setting up shop every weekend now."

"Yeah, but those places usually have skinny-girl stuff. We've established that I'm—"

"Stop. You are beautiful. If we don't find something here, we'll go to Amarillo."

She smiled. "You really would do that, wouldn't you?" When was she going to stop being surprised by his charity and selflessness?

"Of course. I wouldn't say it if I didn't mean it."

"My mom…she's hard on me. Any imperfection is like a neon sign."

The realization of what she'd said slowly registered on Bandit's face. "Oh."

"I'll call her back and tell her something came up. We'll both be in the clear." He'd done so much for her; it was time for Skye to rescue him.

Shaking his head, he said, "N-n-o, that's n-n-not right. I'll h-h-handle it."

She stepped in closer. "But you shouldn't have to."

He brushed her hair from her shoulder and ran his hand down her arm until his fingers tangled in hers. "I'll be okay."

It wasn't fair. His dad had walked out on his mom. He'd grown up poor. He'd had all these things that kids shouldn't have to face. The kind of things that made people angry and bitter.

And yet, here was Bandit. With every right in the world to hold a jaded view of life, he was loving and generous.

"Okay," Skye replied and smiled. "If she messes with you, I might get ugly."

"You couldn't get ugly if you tried."

She hugged his bicep and looked up at him. "Come on, sweet talker. Let's check out those clothes you told me about."

His cheeks bloomed pink, and he shook his head. Instead of responding, he started walking. It tickled her, but he held it in. Man, he sure was cute. Suddenly, a thought danced through her mind. Bandit was a great guy. So, what was her hang up?

Then it hit her. Robert. But it went so much deeper than she realized. He'd been nice at first too. Boy, had he ever. Her mom loved him enough to make Skye wonder if her mom didn't love him more. Until she'd told her parents she was marrying Bandit, her mom was still encouraging Skye to make amends with Robert. In her mom's defense, Robert was two different people. The one when everyone was looking, and then the other one when they were alone.

She didn't get that vibe from Bandit, but she could've said the same about Robert. She wouldn't have dated him if she had. Even looking back, she couldn't see any signs. How could she trust herself now when she'd been so gullible the first time?

There was also the matter of his fortune to consider. Once they were married for the year, he'd be a billionaire. He'd have his choice of women. She knew he'd say that wasn't true, but it was, and she wasn't...a trophy wife. Not like the kind he'd have flocking to him. Bandit would say he couldn't speak well, but it would be overlooked for that kind of money.

With those sorts of insecurities running around in her head, and then pregnancy hormones added on top of it, no wonder she couldn't figure out if she was coming or going. She needed to work on herself before even thinking about a relationship with Bandit. It was best for them both.

CHAPTER 15

Well, *time to meet the in-laws*, Bandit thought as he cut the truck engine on Thanksgiving Day. They'd arrived early so he could meet her parents and siblings prior to her aunts, uncles, and cousins showing up. Skye thought it would be easier that way when it came to introductions.

On the drive to Amarillo, he'd silently gone over and over the relaxation techniques the therapist suggested. He was comfortable around Skye, which was funny because he'd never been comfortable around anyone. Whatever kindred spirit they shared had to be rather powerful, or so he'd reasoned with himself. It didn't mean they were soul mates, just...friends.

Set back from the road with a semicircle driveway,

her parents' two-story brick home with a manicured lawn was like something he'd see in a magazine. It had an air to it like it was to be treated like a museum rather than a home. Then again, it could've been his talks with Skye that made him feel that way. The house wasn't exactly obnoxious, but they were well-off and it showed.

Bandit learned about it during one of their first conversations after meeting at the restaurant. She didn't want him to think she was a gold digger or something. Her parents had wanted her to join the family construction business, but she'd struck out on her own. She and her mom had a disagreement, and she was cut off. She told him she wasn't receiving anything to start with; it was more symbolic than anything. The relationship with her mom was strained, and that was putting it mildly according to Skye.

She exhaled heavily and groaned. "I guess it's now or never." She looked at him. "You know, we can still escape, right? I mean, it's completely okay with me."

Shaking his head, he laughed. So far, she'd tried to offer up all the reasons they couldn't or shouldn't go—but most of them surrounded him and his speech. Each time he'd politely declined. If what Skye said about her mother was true, he knew it was going to be a long day. They were her family, though, and he wasn't going to be the excuse used to stand in the way of her spending time with her family.

The day spent at the farmer's market eased the awkwardness of the kiss they'd shared, and by the time they'd returned home, things were somewhat back to normal. Not totally, though. Bandit couldn't pinpoint a reason, but in his spirit, he knew something was off. The feeling he had kept him from asking too.

"Maybe it won't be so bad. You've got that pretty sweater dress on and your hair curled." Boy, did Skye shine. When she'd first walked out of the bathroom, he was flat-out stunned. He'd thought she was pretty before, but he didn't know he was living with a beauty queen. "She's gonna take one look at you and think you're the prettiest girl on the planet, just like I do."

Her cheeks flamed red, and she ducked her head. "It makes my butt look big." Then she chuckled, and he knew exactly what she was thinking.

"Oh, no, I'm not falling for that again." He shook his finger at her.

She snickered. "Why do you have to spoil my fun?"

Instead of responding, he opened the door of the pickup and stepped out to jog to the passenger side. He reached her just in time to help her down. So far, he'd hadn't figured out why she didn't wait on him anymore.

"You don't have to help me down. I'm more than capable of getting out of the truck." She leveled her eyes at him.

"My mom said it was a sign of respect, and my grandpa said he'd haunt me if I didn't open doors for women." He flashed her the cheesiest grin in his toolbox.

It earned him a pop on the bicep and a roll of the eyes. "Goofball."

She smoothed out her dress and fussed with her hair. "I really don't want to be here."

Taking her by the shoulders, he caught her gaze and held it. "I know you don't. I know you've been pretty beat-up in the past, but I wasn't here. I will not let anyone disrespect you or hurt you. I don't care who they are." The words had flowed smoothly. It seemed like anytime it came to fighting for her, his mouth could work just fine.

For a moment, all she did was stare at him. Just as he was about to apologize, she replied, "I don't know what to say."

Whew. While he would have apologized—for the forcefulness of his words—he still would've done exactly what he said he would. His job was to protect her, real wife or not. "Good." He held out his hand and splayed his fingers. "Ready to face this together?"

Nodding, she smiled and linked her fingers in his. "For once, I think so."

As they walked to the door, she said, "Now, not sure what you've had at your Thanksgivings, but here we have pernil and turkey, rice and beans, papas, my dad's grandmother's aunt's famous fruitcake, and flan."

"I thought fruitcake was for Christmas."

Skye snorted. "Oh, it'll still be sitting like a rock in your stomach at Christmas. That's why Mom sets it out now."

He grimaced. "That bad, huh?"

"Oh yeah," she said as they reached the door. Her finger was almost on the button—which struck him as odd that she'd need to do that, but it didn't matter—when the door swung wide and a woman a lot older-looking than Mrs. Alvarez stood there. Skye squealed, "Abuelita!"

The two women embraced and swayed from side to side. "My sweet Skye."

"I had no idea you were going to be here." They seemed to squeeze each other tighter. One of Bandit and Skye's conversations had revealed that her grand-mother, her dad's mom, was a retired school teacher who was now a novelist living in Belize so she could research their ancestry.

The older woman leaned back and held Skye's face in her hands. "Oh, you just get more beautiful every time I see you."

Bandit held back a laugh. "S-s-see I told y-y-you so." When was he going to learn that those stupid relaxation things didn't work?

Skye scoffed. "Abuelita, this is Bandit. Bandit, this is my Abuelita."

In the next second, Bandit was wrapped in Skye's grandma's arms. "Oh, it's good to meet you."

"She's never really met a stranger," Skye said. It came out almost like an apology.

Shrugging, Bandit shook his head, hoping to convey without words that it was okay. He didn't mind being hugged. It's just what grandmas do.

Her grandma was focused on Skye again. "Come in, come in. Your dad and brother should be back pretty quickly. They just ran out to get some whipped cream. Jen is running late, but she'll be here later."

Bandit followed as he pulled his Stetson from his head and shut the door behind him. The house was just as grand on the inside as it was on the outside. A spiral staircase hugged the wall that led to a balcony. Overhead, a massive chandelier hung where the light coming through the skylight hit it, sending little flecks of light everywhere. The floors looked to be old wood, much like the reclaimed wood in Bear's ranch house. A few feet from the door, a bank of windows allowed him to see an ornate corner desk and wide leather office chair.

"W-w-wow." Bandit didn't even realize he'd said it until Skye took his hand, pulling him farther into the expansive home which only seemed to get grander. Now that he was in the house, the inside was giving the outside a run for its money when it came to opulence.

Waving to the couch, Skye's grandma said, "Now, your mom said you have a story to tell?"

A moment later, a woman appeared at the far end of the living room. Her shoulders were pulled back, her head was held high, and she had the expression of a high school principal who's just caught someone spray-painting the brand-new mural.

As she approached them, she smiled. "Well, you did surprise me, Skye." She perched on a chair between two couches that faced each other. "Your dress is an interesting color." Her gaze traveled from Skye to Bandit. "And you must be the husband." Each sentence held a twinge of condescension that hit Bandit the wrong way. If he weren't meeting this woman for the first time, he'd already be telling her to watch her tone.

Skye went rigid, indicating she seemed to take them the same way he did. She replied, "He is."

Her grandma's mouth dropped open. "Married?"

"Y-y-yes, ma'am. Th-th-that's m-m-me." He closed his eyes and internally chastised himself. Skye took his hand in between hers. Taking a deep breath, he opened his eyes and smiled.

"He's nervous," Skye said.

"Is this the first time you've been here?" Abuelita asked.

As if on cue, Doreen's lips quirked up. "Oh, yes, that's a long story."

Skye swallowed hard. "It's not that long. You know about Robert leaving me, and that I was pregnant."

Her grandma nodded.

"Well, Bandit's grandpa died a few months ago, and part of his will was making sure Bandit got married. We have a mutual friend, and she introduced us." She glanced at him and smiled.

"And he's paying her to stay with him until next year," her mom added.

Abuelita's gaze drifted from Skye to Doreen, landed on Bandit a fraction of a second, and then moved back to Skye. A thick silence settled over the room, and Bandit wanted to disappear. "Is that true, Skye?"

"It is, but it wasn't that simple. His grandpa said he'd forfeit his inheritance if he didn't get married. And it's not just about the money for him. His grandpa has businesses and charities that receive money. If he hadn't married, all that money would've stopped. Bandit didn't have a choice, and he only had a little over sixty days."

The woman's gaze returned to Bandit. "Sixty days."

Nodding, he said, "Y-y-yes, ma'am. H-h-he was a-a-afraid...I d-d-don't like the w-w-way I talk. I t-t-told him I d-d-didn't want to g-g-get m-m-married." Her expression gave him no clue to what she might be thinking. If there was a hole he could crawl into, he'd do it.

Longer than he liked, she remained stoic, until a tiny smile lifted her lips. "I would have liked your grandpa."

Bandit couldn't have heard her right. "Wh-wh-what?"

"A man who gives his fortune away is a good man. A man willing to give up everything is a grandfather who loves his grandson. A grandson who cares enough to honor an outlandish request to continue his grandfather's legacy is a man who is willing to put other's needs ahead of his own." She pointed at Bandit. "And *that* is the measure of a man."

With a sniff, Skye lowered her gaze to the floor. "Stupid hormones," she mumbled just loud enough for him to hear.

Doreen huffed. "You can't possibly think this is a good idea."

"I think it's a lovely idea." She glared at Skye's mom. "Have you two considered staying married once the year is up?"

This family didn't mince words at all. Bandit hadn't been sure how it would feel meeting Skye's family, but he hadn't expected their agreement to be thrown down in the middle and discussed the second they got in the door. It was her grandma, though, and he knew from spending time with his grandpa that older folks tackled things head-on. At least, the ones he knew.

Skye sucked in a sharp breath. "I have a flower shop."

"And a baby." Her grandma chuckled. "Are you okay with that?" She directed the question to Bandit.

He nodded and smiled as she held his gaze. "Y-y-yes, ma'am. M-m-more th-th-than okay." If he could speak better, he'd say more than that. Even now, knowing the relationship would come to an end, he desperately wanted to be the father. If he met someone else down the road, which was unlikely, they'd have to understand that Skye's baby was his baby too.

Skye's grandma grinned wider as if she'd read his mind. "See, he's a good man." Her nose wrinkled. "I never did like that Robert."

Doreen huffed. "He was an upstanding citizen. He's the CFO of—"

"And he left her!" The older woman rolled her eyes. "Do you know what you're having yet?" she asked Skye. Bandit suspected she was trying to diffuse the stressful situation.

Shaking her head, Skye grinned. "No, I want it to be a surprise."

The front door opened. "Mama!" a male voice boomed from the front of the house. "We have the whipped cream." Instantly, stress flowed out of the room like wine from a broken barrel.

Skye's grandma stood. "In here, my heart."

Bandit almost sighed in relief at the sound of Mr. Alvarez's voice. For the moment at least, the focus was off Bandit. He suspected it would return soon. The man was Skye's father after all. Still, it gave him a second to catch his breath.

He didn't know what to think about Skye's grandma suggesting they stay married. Of course, it was something he'd thought about more than once. If

Skye would consider it. He could sacrifice his cabin at the ranch if she wanted to stay in Amarillo and run her shop. Or better, maybe they could open a place like they'd talked about that night as they watched the stars.

It was certainly something to consider, and if he could find his courage, maybe he'd ask. He'd just need to prepare himself if the answer was no. The thought made his heart ache. As much as he wanted to be okay either way, he wasn't going to be. He'd fallen for her, and it had been the easiest thing he'd ever done.

CHAPTER 16

Hiding was cowardly, but at the moment, Skye didn't care. The study she'd tucked herself away in was the farthest away from all the festivities happening downstairs. Abuelita was there, so she knew Bandit would be okay for a little bit. Just long enough for her to get her emotions under control.

Why had she bothered to dress up? She'd known it wouldn't matter what she wore, how she fixed her hair, or anything else. Her mom would have something negative to say. That's how she'd always been, and nothing was ever going to change that.

Then looking at Bandit like he was dirt because of the way he spoke? At least Abuelita had come to the rescue before Skye opened her mouth and ruined

Thanksgiving. While she didn't like the digs directed at her, Skye could grit her teeth and deal with it. Bandit, on the other hand, she was ready to go to war for him. It most likely would have ended the holiday with her storming out with him in tow.

"You know sequestering yourself has never fixed anything," Jen said.

Skye pulled her gaze from the study window and found her sister in the doorway. Of course, she'd look like perfection with immaculately coifed hair and makeup. And the flowy blouse and navy slacks fit the image of a successful woman to a T.

With the study being so far from the front door, it made sense that Jen's arrival had happened without Skye knowing it. "No, but it does give me a chance to stew and regroup." Her relationship with her sister was decent. She didn't see her much because Jen lived in Houston. She'd taken the news about Bandit better than their mom and dad. Of course, the shock was exactly the same.

Jen crossed the room, pulling Skye into an embrace. "I've missed you." She leaned back. "No matter what Mom says, you look fantastic."

Rolling her eyes, Skye scoffed. "Right."

"You do." Jen stepped back, leaning her shoulder against the wall. "Don't let Mom get to you."

"Easy for you to say, Ms. Perfect." Skye didn't mean the words to come out so sharp. "I'm sorry. I know it's not you. It's just...nothing I do is ever good enough, and I'm tired of it."

Her sister crossed her arms over her chest as her gaze dipped to the floor. "Have you ever thought about just saying that? Just laying it all out on the table?"

She'd tried that a few years ago, and it had changed nothing. "I have."

"Really? When? Because all I've ever seen is you two arguing. Screaming 'Nothing is ever good enough!' as you storm out of the house isn't telling her how you feel. It's running away. You need to tell her." Jen lifted her head and met Skye's gaze. "Don't blow up. Just calmly say how you feel."

There may have been a little truth to what her sister was saying. Plus, if Skye were honest with herself, it was more than a few years ago. It was more like just after she'd graduated high school. "Maybe," she said softly. "What if I do lay out my feelings and nothing changes?"

"Then it'll be on Mom. If she knows how you feel and still does it, you can reevaluate then."

"I just wish I didn't have to." Skye sighed.

"I know, but you do." Jen took a deep breath and let

it out slowly. A change of topics was coming. "Abuelita likes Bandit."

Nodding, Skye smiled. "Yeah, she does."

Jen laughed. "He's a lot different than Robert. Cuter too."

Heat rushed to Skye's cheeks. "Yeah, he is."

"I think you were settling for Robert. That's why you put up with him." Jen gave Skye a pointed look.

She hadn't put her feelings into those exact words, but that was the conclusion Skye was leaning toward. "I think so too."

"Well, finally."

"What?" Skye asked. "I thought you liked him."

Her lips twisted in disgust. "Polite doesn't mean I like someone. Polite means I'm not going to punch them in the mouth. He was a jerk who thought the world revolved around him."

Skye's jaw dropped. "Really?"

"Yeah, really. He was slimy, and I always had a weird vibe from him. I wouldn't be surprised to find out he didn't leave you because you were pregnant. More like he was running from the police or something for investment fraud. He was seriously shady."

The microscope Skye was using for her past relationship absolutely backed that feeling up. She'd ignored so many things about Robert.

"Now, Bandit, on the other hand, seems as genuine as they come. And I'll be honest, I came in today wanting to not like him."

Rolling her eyes, Skye huffed and chuckled. "Why would you come to Thanksgiving wanting to dislike him?"

"Like it's an everyday occurrence that people get married because a will tells them to? Just how awful would you have to be?"

"All right, I'll give you that." Which was another reason she wasn't rushing into anything with Bandit. So far, her grandma and sister liked him, but that didn't mean Skye shouldn't be careful.

"He's nothing like I expected. Tall, head full of hair, muscled. The guy's a flat-out stud." Jen snorted and jerked her hands to her face to cover her nose.

Skye squeaked as she tried to hold in a laugh. Snorting was the one thing they shared, only Jen was better at controlling it most of the time. Skye rolled her lips in and then busted it out.

"Shut up!" Jen gently pushed on her shoulder. "Of all the things I could inherit from Dad, it had to be this?"

"Better than his ugly toes." Still laughing, Skye straightened. "Okay, I guess I'm ready to face the world again. Plus, I don't want to abandon Bandit to the wolves for too long."

Jen linked her arm through one of Skye's. "Aunt Theresa brought her sweet-potato casserole this year."

"The one with the walnut-and-brown-sugar topping?"

"That's the one." Jen grinned.

Skye moaned. "Oh, it was so good. When she didn't bring it last year, I nearly cried."

"You and me both."

By the time they made it to the first floor, Jen had filled her in on just about everything going on downstairs. The one thing Skye wasn't sad to have missed was their third cousin Wilson. He'd received a hair transplant and was having everyone pull on it to show how real it was. Just the thought made Skye a little queasy. She made a pact with Jen that if either of them caught him approaching, there would be a sudden reason they had to leave.

After a few short hellos to the family who had arrived, Skye left Jen in search of Bandit, finding him in the kitchen at the large granite-top island with Abuelita, working on homemade bread.

One of the reasons her mom had loved the house was this feature. Not only did it have a sink, but it had electrical outlets and enough space to roll out whatever doughy food her mom wanted to cook.

Leaning against the kitchen doorframe, she silently watched him work. He was nothing like Robert. No way would he have been caught doing anything of the sort. Not even close. Comparing Bandit to Robert was more like an insult, really.

Skye *had* settled for Robert, and while she'd become more critical of their relationship since he'd left, she'd never put it exactly in those terms. The question she found herself asking was why? Had she really felt that she couldn't do better? Robert had sure made it known that was how he felt, but why did Skye simply accept that as the truth?

Sure, she wanted to be loved, but at what cost? As much as it hurt that she'd been abandoned, she was now seeing it as a good thing that he'd left. Those months, cooped up in her townhome, hiding from the world, she'd cried her eyes out over what she thought she'd lost.

No more. She was done looking back and wishing she could change things. Instead, she was taking her newfound insight about herself and making changes so she could move on. No more Robert. That relationship was done and over.

It didn't mean she wanted or intended to jump into

another relationship, but it did solidify that whatever her future held, it was wholly dependent on her and her attitude.

Whether her destiny involved Bandit or not, that was to be seen. All she knew was that she wasn't going to allow her yesterdays to cloud her tomorrows.

CHAPTER 17

With all the aunts, uncles, and cousins, Bandit's idea of a small Thanksgiving had vanished. He wasn't sure why he'd only expected it to be Skye's immediate family. She'd told him more than once that their family held a huge feast for Thanksgiving—which, now that he'd experienced a holiday with her family, felt more like a family reunion than a holiday.

It got to him a little, all the noise and new people. The Wests were a large family as well. With everyone marrying and having children, it only seemed to grow with each passing year. The difference was that he'd grown up with them. He could handle the holidays with them. Skye's family took a little more work.

When Skye first excused herself to the restroom,

he knew it wasn't just a bathroom break. He could see in her eyes that her mom had hurt her feelings, and then Abuelita suggesting they stay together had made her uncomfortable. While it didn't bother him, he knew Skye didn't want a relationship and she'd felt put on the spot. He couldn't fault her for escaping a minute.

A light bump to the arm interrupted his thoughts. Pausing the kneading of the dough he was working on, he chose to smile at Abuelita instead of speaking.

"Oh, don't you pull that with me." Skye's grandma shook her finger at him. "I taught school for years. You aren't the first boy I've ever heard stutter."

Her tone was stern, not harsh. More matter-of-fact than anything as an assurance that his speech didn't bother her. "I kn-kn-know."

She turned, leaning her back against the counter as she crossed her arms over her chest. "You might not believe this, but you're the only one who cares about your stuttering."

He wanted to believe that, but how could it not bother other people? It took him what seemed like forever to get an entire sentence out. Shaking his head, he replied, "N-n-not s-s-sure I b-b-believe you."

Laying her hand on his arm, she said, "You should." Her eyes narrowed, for a moment, and he thought she was going to argue with him. Instead, she faced the counter, and he began to pinch off dough to make rolls.

Once the last batch of rolls was in the oven, she fixed them some coffee and asked him to keep her company on the porch. For the end of November, it was comfortable with a coat on.

Bandit thought for sure she'd be asking him a ton of questions, but instead, they fell into a comfortable silence watching birds land in the spacious backyard. Smoke trailed from the few houses he could see, and the scent of mesquite and hickory filled the air. His ears were a little chilly, but he enjoyed the peace too much to go inside.

Just as he finished his coffee and set the cup on the deck beside his chair, Skye's grandma cleared her throat. He silently braced himself for whatever line of questioning was coming.

Abuelita angled herself toward him. "So, tell me more about this grandpa of yours."

That was an easy subject. It took more time than he liked, but he told her how his grandpa learned of his existence, how he'd tracked Bandit down, and how they'd become friends before his death. Talking about it still hurt Bandit's heart.

"When my husband passed away, I thought I'd

wither and follow him a few months later. Then the days turned to weeks and the weeks to months." She paused, taking a sip of her coffee. "It's been a little over seven years, and I still miss him."

"H-h-how long were y-y-you married?"

A smile quirked on her lips. "We got married when I was seventeen. Our anniversary, had he lived another month, would have made it forty-five years."

"L-l-long time."

"Not nearly as long as I would have liked." She smiled. "But I'm grateful for the years we had."

Rubbing the spot over his heart, Bandit felt the ache of that statement, both for his mom and his grandpa. When he'd thought about marriage, the few times he had allowed himself, he'd wanted years and years of loving someone. Marrying Skye with a contract in place had made him feel disgusting, especially now that he was wishing there could be more between them.

"You know, just because you have a contract doesn't mean it has to end. As long as the two parties involved agree to the change, the contract is satisfied."

"You j-j-just met m-m-me. What if I'm g-g-good at foolin' p-p-people?" He wasn't, but how could Skye's grandma be so sure?

Shaking her head, she crossed her arms over her

chest. "I know." She squared her shoulders. "Plus, I googled your grandfather. I'm old, not technologically challenged."

Bandit leaned his head against the back of the chair as he laughed. The only other person to make him laugh that hard was Skye. "I kn-kn-know where Skye g-g-gets her humor."

Abuelita's hand came to rest on his forearm. "I saw how you looked at her. You care deeply for her."

He started to shake his head, and she cut him off. "I know you two haven't known each other for all that long, but sometimes you don't have to. Every once in a while, two people meet and that's all she wrote. I don't know why it works that way other than those two people had souls who were looking for each other long before they knew it."

"S-s-she isn't w-w-wanting to be in a r-r-relationship."

"Oh, hogwash. I saw how she looked at you too. She's just as smitten."

As sweet as that thought was, it wasn't true. She looked at him like a friend and nothing more. Her grandma wanted to see something that wasn't there. "I'm s-s-sorry, but n-n-no."

No sooner had the last word left his lips, and the door opened. "You two hiding out here?"

Bandit turned, grateful Skye hadn't been a minute earlier. "N-n-no. Just v-v-visiting."

"Well, you have about two minutes left on the rolls before the timer goes off." She took a few more steps toward Bandit, and he stood.

Before he could offer to get them, Abuelita jumped up. "I'll get them." She hurried inside, leaving him alone with Skye.

Skye took a few more steps, closing most of the gap between them. "I'm sorry for ditching you earlier."

"It's okay. You needed a second."

"I shouldn't. I should be old enough to deal with things like an adult. My mom just tongue-ties me." She hugged herself. "Jen said I need to tell her how I feel."

"That's not bad advice." He smiled. "Actually, it might work wonders."

With a heavy sigh, she dropped her arms to her sides. "You two make it sound so easy. I just..."

"You're afraid of telling her and it not making a difference. If you don't say anything, you can hide behind it and hold on to hope that if you did, she'd change. If she doesn't, then it'll mean she knows it hurts and doesn't care."

She jerked her gaze to his. "You're supposed to be on my side."

"I am. We all hide behind something."

"Like stuttering?" Her posture softened, and she wrapped her arms around his waist, setting her chin on his chest. "Your worth isn't tied to your speech, ya know?"

"And your worth isn't tied to your mother's opinion," he said, circling his arms around her. "Or Robert's."

Rolling her eyes, she chuckled. "We sure are a pair, huh?"

"I can handle that pairing." He pulled her to him and kissed the top of her head. "This is good."

He loosened his hold on her, took her shoulders in his hands, and leaned back. Being alone with her gave him ideas he didn't need to act on. "You ready to go back inside?"

"If I say no, will you stay out here with me?"

With a laugh, he nodded. "I'll stay, but I'm not sure my ears can handle it."

Skye took her arms from around him, sliding her hands up his chest until she was covering them. "You've got little icebergs there."

In an instant, their casual embrace turned from easy and comfortable to electric. All the talk of staying together and Abuelita's thoughts on the way they looked at each other filled his mind. It was all just talk. Risky too. There was no way she cared about or could care about him like that.

Just as he thought his heart and head had come to an understanding, his lips broke the truce and touched hers. He hadn't thought it possible that her lips could be softer than the last time, but they were. Sweeter, fuller, and more wonderful than before.

Instead of pushing him away, her hands slipped behind his neck and pulled him closer. The slow, soft kisses grew faster as the need for her increased.

Taking his hat from his head, he used it to shield them as he deepened the kiss with the last touch of their lips. This moment was theirs, and he wasn't sharing it with her family.

Their hurried, feverish kisses continued and eventually slowed as they changed from need to something deeper than he'd ever experienced. It felt like his soul was begging for her. All of him needed all of her. He could live a thousand years and need her just as much as right at that moment.

The languid, scorching kisses came to a stop, and she touched her forehead to his chin.

The last time she'd kissed him, she hadn't wanted to talk about it. She'd said it was a mistake. Part of him wanted to ask her if she still felt that way, but fear of the answer kept him from asking.

Once he'd taken a few gulps of air, he set his hat back on his head. "I guess we should get inside, huh?"

She pulled back a fraction, her breath mingling with his. "I guess so."

Cupping her cheek, he stroked her swollen lips with his thumb, fighting with everything he had not to kiss her again. "Okay." He tangled his fingers in hers and led her to the door.

For now, he'd keep his thoughts on the kiss to himself and spend time with her. That was good enough...for the moment.

DINNER WITH SKYE'S family was a wholly different experience than a meal with the Wests, especially since he wasn't in the kitchen. Everything was delicious, and he enjoyed being just a person at the dinner table. The previous Thanksgiving he'd spent with his grandfather, and they'd gone to a diner that his grandpa loved. Bandit didn't cook, but the feeling was different from this. Maybe it was the number of people who changed it.

Shortly after the meal was over and the dishes were done, Skye's dad and brother invited him to play cornhole in the backyard. He'd expected her father would want to have a talk at some point. The fact that it had happened later rather than sooner was surprising.

"Yo, Bandit, it's your turn," Andy called.

Bandit startled from where he was leaning against a large oak tree and straightened. "Sorry."

He took his spot at the throwing line, squinted, and let the corn-filled bag fly. He wondered if basketball players felt the thrill of a slam dunk the same way he did when he sank a bag without touching the hole.

"Sheesh," Skye's dad, Mike, said. "If I'd known you were this good, I'd have suggested something else."

"Right?" Andy, her brother, nodded in agreement. "How'd you get so good at this?"

Shrugging, Bandit shook his head. He'd spent most of the day speaking as little as possible. "D-d-don't kn-kn-know."

Mike touched his son's shoulder. "Hey, man, would you go inside and get us something to drink? I want to talk to Bandit a minute." Yep, right on time.

Andy looked from his dad to Bandit and smiled. "Sure, Dad. I'll be back in a second."

As soon as he was in the house, Mike turned to Bandit. It felt like an eternity as the man seemed to size him up. Her dad crossed his arms over his chest. "I have no idea what Skye was thinking by agreeing to marry a man for money. The craziest thing I've ever heard."

Yeah, Bandit had to agree with the statement, but he didn't like the tone. What little time he'd had to observe them before her extended family began arriving, his relationship with Skye was a complete contrast to her mom. She was Daddy's little girl from what Bandit could tell.

"That's what she gets for being single and pregnant. Her weight doesn't help either." Mike shook his head. "I told her if she didn't start dressing better and taking care of herself, she—"

"Now you listen here," Bandit growled. "You're her father, and I mean no disrespect, but you will not speak of her like that." His heart took the wheel from his brain. "Skye is perfect the way she is. Weight or not, she is a beautiful woman. Her baby is precious and loved. If she'll allow me to be the father, I will take that responsibility willingly. She will always have me to lean on if she needs anything." Bandit pulled up straight, his shoulders back. "Don't *ever* let me hear you speaking of her like that again." Once Bandit's little speech was over, he was shocked how quickly and clearly he'd spoken. Apparently, when it came to anything Skye, his head, heart, and mouth were on the same page.

For a moment, he faced off with Skye's dad, and slowly the man began to chuckle. "Momma said you were a good man. I just had to check for myself."

"Wh-wh-what?"

"I said that same thing to Robert when I met him, and that sorry excuse for a man agreed with me. Skye never knew because she can be hard-headed, but I hated that jerk." He scoffed. "Can you believe that idiot actually thought I'd give him a job at our company?"

"A j-j-job?" Skye never mentioned that. It was possible she didn't know.

"Yeah, like somehow marrying Skye would magically make me like him. I was going to talk to her about it when she called to tell us he'd split." Mike dropped his arms to his sides. "I would have told her, but she was so hurt, and I didn't want to pile on more heartbreak." He shook his head. "In my mind, the best thing he ever did for her was leave. Not only will she be better off, but the baby will too."

They certainly shared that feeling. "He w-w-wasn't much of a m-m-man."

"Nope, but you're all right." Sticking his hand out to Bandit, Mike smiled. "Welcome to the family, buddy."

The back door slammed shut, and Andy

approached them carrying three bottles of soda. "Did he pass?"

"Flying colors." His dad snagged one and twisted the top off, taking a long swing. He tipped his head toward his son. "I told him what I'd done when we met Robert. That's why neither of us liked him. I would have told Skye, but I felt like if I did, she'd just think I was being overprotective."

Andy passed a drink to Bandit. "We tried to tell my mom, but she thought Dad was just being Dad."

"She's stubborn just like Skye." Mike shrugged. "What can I say?"

Bandit held his tongue. Skye's mom came across as hateful and judgmental—not just about Skye's pregnancy, but everything.

Andy knocked Bandit's arm with his elbow. "Skye will come around."

"She will," Mike said. "I'll make sure of it."

"We're o-o-only going to be t-t-together a year." Bandit hated how it sounded and, even worse, how it felt to say it.

Mike exchanged a look with Andy. Immediately, Bandit knew without a doubt that they'd spied him sharing a kiss with Skye, and he braced for whatever they might say about it. He almost wanted to make an excuse for it, but he couldn't and wouldn't lie.

"Yeah, but until then, you're family." Her dad held his gaze as he said it. Almost if he shared the same thoughts as his mother.

After a few rounds of cornhole, the consensus was that it was too cold to continue, and they went back inside. Had Bandit realized why, he might have protested a bit. Fruitcake, and from the short glance he'd had as they walked through the kitchen, it looked awful. There weren't enough tubs of cool whip or whipped cream made to fix what ailed it.

"Did my dad give you grief?" Skye asked softly.

Her dad and grandma were in the kitchen getting the cake sliced while the rest of the family was hanging out in the living room near the fireplace. With as big as the room was, the fire inside made it warm and not oppressive. Still, the sleeves on Skye's sweater dress were shoved up to her elbows.

Leaning in, he whispered back, "I like your dad." His method was unorthodox, but it was a good way to gauge a person's character. A dad had to make sure the man his daughter was spending her time with was worthy of that time. Bandit was mighty grateful he'd received her dad's approval, for however short a time it was.

Little whispers from the back of his mind roared. He'd been thinking...wondering if he could convince her to stay with him. If he didn't have her grandma—and if he wasn't mistaken, her dad too—adding to those pesky little hopes, maybe he could have buried them deeper.

They didn't have to be an actual married couple. It would be so the baby had a stable home with a mother and a father. He wasn't saying she couldn't be a fantastic single mom, but was it wrong to offer her an alternative? He couldn't see the downside.

Well, other than a broken heart, but he could handle that. He'd dealt with much worse, and she was a whole lot prettier to look at.

CHAPTER 18

That fruitcake had hit Skye's stomach like a brick launched off a skyscraper. The slice she'd been handed from her grandma was larger than normal since she was eating for two. Only the baby didn't like it any more than she did. He'd been kicking her in a sensitive place since the first bite. The little tyrant's way of getting back at her.

After pacing the kitchen a few times, she stopped and arched her back to alleviate some of the discomfort. When that didn't help, she walked to the table, braced her hands on a chair back, and tried stretching again.

"You all right?" Bandit asked.

Glancing over her shoulder, she nodded. "Yeah, just achy."

He tossed his plate into the trash bin and joined her at the table. "You sure? You look a little pale."

"I can't get comfortable, and I feel weird." She grimaced.

One of his arms wrapped around her waist, and he palmed her cheek. "I think you should see a doctor."

She smiled. "I think I'll be okay."

In one swift motion, he pulled his hand free of her face and swept it under her legs, lifting her off her feet. "I know you'll be okay because I'm taking you to the doctor."

"What's going on?" her mom barked.

"She doesn't feel good, and she's hurting. I'm taking her to the doctor." His voice was as smooth and firm as Skye had ever heard.

"Skye?"

"I think he's right," Skye replied, sucking in a sharp breath as a sharper pain sliced through her abdomen.

Her mom flew across the room. "We should call an ambulance."

Bandit shook his head. "I can get her there faster."

With that, he strode past her mom and through the house, and by the time he made it to the truck, her dad was there to open the door. Bandit set her in the seat and leaned it back. He turned to her family. "Mrs. Alvarez, you want to ride with us?"

All Skye heard was the squeak of a *yes* and the sound of the door opening and shutting. The next second, Bandit was leaning over her. "Your momma is with us, and I'm gonna get you there as quickly as I can."

"Okay."

Her mom sat on the edge of her seat, her fingers raking through Skye's hair and whispering encouragement. When they reached the hospital, Bandit was out of the truck and picking her up, rushing her through the doors of the emergency room.

It wasn't until he was placing her on a bed that she realized he'd picked her up twice. Her. Forty-pounds-overweight-and-pregnant her. She half expected to see him in a bed next to her with a broken back.

Several tests later, it was determined that she'd experienced a mild case of Braxton Hicks contractions, only there wasn't anything false about them. And if those were their idea of mild, she'd eat a Brussel sprout. Her blood pressure was a little too high for the doctor's liking too. She told him about the fruitcake and her Abuelita's heart breaking if she didn't eat the horrible confection, but he laughed at her. He laughed even harder when she threatened to bring him a slice as an offer of proof.

From what she could tell, it wasn't all that serious.

It was just painful, but she'd been admitted so she could be observed overnight. Mostly that was because of Bandit's insistence. They lived two hours away, and he didn't want to be in the middle of nowhere with not a hospital in sight if something else happened.

As soon as they got her in the room, her mom was there, fussing over her while Bandit visited the gift shop. "Is there anything I can get you?"

"No, I'm okay."

"I'm glad Bandit insisted you stay the night. He was right about being so far away from the hospital. Maybe it would be a good idea if you stayed at the house. That way, if anything else happened, you'd be close."

"Now that I know what false labor feels like, I doubt I'll need to come back until it's the real thing." She chuckled.

Her mom fidgeted with the bed covers a little and then perched on the edge beside Skye. "I'm just glad you and the baby are okay."

A small sniff from her mom caught Skye off guard. Her mom held one of Skye's hands between hers. "You scared the dickens out of me. All I could think of was the times I'd been critical of you. That's not how I want things to be. You looked great today, and I was petty. You deserved better from me. I'm supposed to be the one person you can come to when you're hurting, and I wasn't."

There weren't many times when Skye was speechless, but there wasn't a word she could form that could convey how utterly stunned she was. It took two for a relationship, though, and for her part, she hadn't been Daughter of the Year. "I haven't exactly been the best either. I shouldn't be so disrespectful or hateful."

Her mom patted her hand and then squeezed it. "Maybe, but I'm not winning Mother of the Year anytime soon. All I can say is that I'm deeply sorry for being so judgmental. I will work on being better. There are no excuses for the way I've treated you."

Skye pulled her mom into a hug. "I'm sorry too." She closed her eyes, and tears trickled down her cheeks.

"I've missed so many things. I'm so sorry." She wrapped her arms around Skye and held her tightly.

"Wow. Never would've thought I'd walk in on you two hugging."

They startled, and Skye couldn't believe her eyes as the embrace with her mom ended. "Robert? What are you doing here?"

"Apparently, you haven't taken me off your emergency-contact list." He shrugged. "I figured I'd come see what the fuss was all about." His eyes widened as his gaze raked from her head to her belly. "Wow, you're huge."

Her mom stood and walked around the end of the bed, stopping in front of Skye like a shield. "My daughter has no desire to see you."

Robert shoved his hands in his pockets. "Maybe, but I'd like to talk to her for a minute."

"No."

Skye sighed. "It's okay. I'll be fine."

Glancing over her shoulder, her mom's lips pinched together like she was about to argue. "Are you sure?"

"Yeah, I'm sure. Maybe you should go find Bandit. He said he was going to the gift shop, and I'm not sure what sort of trouble he can get into down there." She offered a smile to color the statement with confidence.

"All right," she said and pulled her shoulders back. As she passed Robert, she looked down her nose at him. "Keep it short."

Robert rolled his eyes and leisurely walked to Skye. "Are you okay?"

That's all he had to say? After months of nothing? "You left me and gave me no reason why. So why are you here?"

He gave her a small one-shoulder shrug. "I don't know. Maybe I just wanted to see you." He smiled.

"You divorced me without so much as a word." Skye pinched the bridge of her nose. Any moment now, a nurse would be returning to check her blood pressure. It was a test she'd fail miserably if he didn't leave. "Just leave me alone."

He glanced over his shoulder at the door and stepped a little closer, lowering his voice. "You think I'm not aware that you're already married again?"

Jerking her gaze to Robert's, she said, "What?"

Rolling his eyes, he scoffed. "I have friends at the courthouse, and you know this. From what I found out, that guy you married is loaded. Stop acting like you're shocked."

"Why would they care?" Yeah, if there ever was a sign from heaven that it was a good thing he walked out, it was this. *You left me.*

"Doesn't mean I don't want to know what you're up to, especially when you're walking around with my kid." Leaning in, his lips curled into a snarl. "You really think that rich guy you married wants you? I mean, look at you. You're not a billionaire's wife."

Her heart dropped to her stomach. First, he knew Bandit had money, and second, he'd cut her in the one place she was the most vulnerable. Whatever confidence she thought she'd built in the weeks prior crumbled.

"You don't know what you're talking about." She spat the words, but even she could hear the lack of confidence in them.

"Don't I? Besides, you're carrying my child. I think I have a right to know what you're doing."

"So? We're divorced. It even says in the papers that you declined *those* rights."

His lips trembled. "Yeah, but I was distraught and afraid. I'm sure a judge would see how that could spook a man, especially when he'd talked to his wife about waiting. That she'd tricked him by telling him she was on birth control."

Her sister thought he was shady, but Skye hadn't taken it as actually underhanded...just that Jen thought he was a sleazeball. "I was. I took it every day. You saw me take it." She took a deep breath and worked her jaw. "What do you want?"

"Depends." He leveled his gaze at her. "How much is this baby worth to you? To him?"

The heart monitor blared as her pulse rocketed and her mouth dropped open. Nothing was making any sense to her. "You want money?"

"With a few hundred thousand, I could be persuaded to just go away." He smiled.

Instinctively, she wrapped her arms around her midsection. Just what was her ex-husband capable of?

"Despite what you might think, we don't have that kind of money."

Robert slipped his hands in his pockets and shrugged. "Maybe. I'm sure you two can think of something. Otherwise, I might have to go to court for custody, or who knows, maybe your new husband will even have an accident." He walked backward a few steps as he held her gaze, his lips curled in a half-smile. "Sorry. I'd stay longer, but I have an appointment with my lawyer. We need to discuss my options for custody." He winked.

The door swung open, and balloons flooded into the room. "Skye!" Bandit stopped short as the space cleared. "What's going on?"

"Robert was just leaving," Skye's mom said, pushing past Bandit.

Robert held up his hands. "Yep. Just needed to make sure she was okay."

Bandit flicked his gaze from Robert to Skye. "She's just fine. Git."

As soon as Robert was gone, whatever had kept her pulled together unraveled, and she covered her face with her hands. As fast as the tears were running down her face, there was no reason to bother trying to wipe them away. Her mind was running a million miles in every direction, working to process the exchange she'd just had with her ex-husband.

In the next minute, Bandit was next to her, gathering her into his arms. "It's okay. Your mom is making sure he isn't allowed to come back."

How could she tell him that her ex had threatened them? Bandit didn't have any money. He'd borrowed money from Bear just to make sure she was comfortable. Robert was asking for hundreds of thousands of dollars. But why? Had he always been like that?

She'd missed so many things with Robert, and even as Bandit held her, knowing the kind of man he was, she couldn't help but wonder if she was overlooking things about him too.

Then there was the issue of his lifestyle. It would change once he was a billionaire. He could say it wouldn't, but that kind of money always changes people. He'd meet women who were much more suited for that lifestyle than Skye. Women who were poised, attractive...thin. What would he want with her then?

Why did she care so much? She'd entered this relationship with no desire to be in one, determined to work on herself before even thinking about it. She needed to raise her child. So many other things she needed more than a relationship.

Her head embraced her heart, and together they answered the question she had. But before she allowed it to even materialize, she squashed it.

It was too soon. She was pregnant, she'd just had a scare, and now she was under stress. It certainly wasn't time to declare or think about...anything.

CHAPTER 19

"Josiah said I'd hear from her as soon as Emilia could call," Bandit said, setting his phone on the nightstand.

One of the perks of being a member of the West family was turning to them when Bandit needed help. As soon as Skye filled him in on Robert's threat, he'd called Josiah and Josiah had called Emilia Sanger, a private detective he'd used when Molly thought they would lose custody of Ellie.

Bandit turned his attention to Skye once again. He'd held her until she'd collected herself enough to speak once Robert was gone. "From what I know, she's the best."

After Skye relayed what happened, her mom and brother had held Mike back from chasing down

Robert and punching his lights out. It was a holiday weekend, and spending it in jail wasn't worth it. That's when the family learned that Robert had come to her dad for a job.

"I knew he was sleazy." Jen chewed the tip of her thumb as she paced the end of Skye's bed. "There was always something off about him."

Abuelita sat in the little recliner in the corner of the room. "I told you I never liked him."

"We know, Mom," Mike replied. "We don't need to rehash it again."

That sort of talk wasn't helping Skye. She'd trusted the man. Loved him and pledged her forever to him. With the exception of her mom, her family hadn't liked him, and they'd kept those feelings from Skye. Something Bandit didn't understand.

"Why didn't you tell me he asked for a job?" Doreen set her hands on her hips. "I should have known that."

"I was going to, but he'd already sent her divorce papers. It never crossed my mind they could be related." He rubbed his face with his hands. "If I'd known…"

Skye's mom softened. "I know. I'm more upset with myself than I am with you. I can't even give a good reason for liking that scum." She turned to Bandit.

"Thank you for calling your family about that private investigator."

He nodded. "You're welcome." No one had mentioned his lack of stuttering so far, but he was certain no one missed it. It made him wonder if Skye's grandma was right all along and he'd been the only one frustrated by it. "I'm told she can find anything."

Andy sat on the bench that lined the wall in front of the window, setting his ankle on his knee. "So, I think the elephant in the room is the money Robert's demanding."

"It's not mine until I've been married a year."

Pushing herself into a sitting position, Skye nodded. "I told him we don't have that kind of money."

Jen stopped pacing and stood behind her parents. "What I don't understand is why he'd want a job with our company. He wouldn't have had access to the sort of money he's demanding."

Doreen palmed her forehead. "If it's the job I told him about, then, yes, he would have."

"You told him?" Skye asked.

"Not like offering him a job, just in passing conversation." She dropped her hand to her side. "Cindy had just put in her two-week notice. I didn't think anything of it."

"Cindy? Wasn't she just your assistant?" Skye asked.

Mike groaned. "Before she was *promoted*. She took care of our vendor accounts. Getting invoices, paying them, keeping them filed. Robert would have had access to one of our bank accounts."

"That certainly makes sense now," Jen added.

"And we know he has a buddy at the bank too," Andy chimed in. "Not saying his friend would be in on it, but if Robert's slimy enough to threaten Skye, then who knows the kind of people he's friends with."

Skye let out a long breath. "I have no idea what he could be mixed up in, and I'm not sure he can really do anything. I'm probably worrying for nothing." That's what her lips said, but her chewed fingernails said otherwise. Her shoulders sagged as a long breath rushed out of her.

Bandit could see the day weighing on her. "I think Skye is tired."

"I'm fine."

Just then, Abuelita met his gaze and smiled. "Well, I'm exhausted." Her grandmother stood. "I think we've all had a long day."

Doreen and Mike nodded. "Yeah, I think that's a good idea. Though, not sure how well I'll sleep," her mom said.

"I don't have anything to wear tomorrow." Skye groaned. "I didn't know I'd be spending the night."

Bandit stood and fished his keys from his pocket, and she latched on to him. "Please don't go."

He smiled as he passed the keys to Jen. "I wasn't going anywhere."

"You're just letting me take your car?"

"Truck, and is there a reason I shouldn't?" Bandit asked, smiling.

"That sounds lovely." Abuelita rubbed her hands together. "I'd love to see Caprock Canyon."

Doreen shrugged. "We could make it a girl's trip."

"House key is the one with the Texas flag on it."

"I think Dad and I need to do a little online fishing." Andy stood and straightened the legs of his jeans. "I'm too curious to just sit around."

A few rounds of goodbyes later, Bandit exhaled. Not that he didn't like Skye's family, but he was weary. Now that he had a chance to take in everything that had transpired, it seemed to sock him in the gut.

The stress of rushing Skye to the hospital and worrying about what could be wrong had been a lot. Her crying out as they took her vitals, vials of blood, and then hooked her up to a labor monitor—which showed she wasn't in labor—had his nerves twisted so tight, it was a wonder he could still think straight.

"You don't have to stay if you don't want to. I was…"

Taking a seat beside her, he shook his head. "I wouldn't leave even if you told me to."

A tiny smile lifted her lips. "You would too."

"Would not."

"Yeah, you would." She laughed. "'Cause you're nice."

He knew she was poking fun at him, but it seemed to lift the strain of the day off her shoulders. If that's what helped her, he didn't mind it. "All right, maybe I would."

She grinned wider. "You haven't been stuttering either."

It wasn't surprising that she'd picked up on that. "No, I haven't been. I realized after you told us what happened that I hadn't since we got to the hospital."

"Really?" she asked as her mouth dropped open. "I mean, not that I care, but I know you care and…" She clamped her lips shut.

"I know what you mean."

"Do you know how or why?"

Yeah, he did. For the first time since his dad left, he felt like he had something to hold on to. During all the chaos, as he helplessly watched Skye, the word love flitted through his mind. Once that happened, his heart was branded. He loved her. Whether or not she ever returned it didn't make it any less true. He wouldn't say anything right now. She was under enough stress as it was. Adding to it would be selfish.

Shrugging, he replied, "I guess I just needed to stop worrying about it."

"Does it make you happier?"

He hadn't really had time to think about, but now that the question was posed, yeah, he was. All the years fretting over it hadn't changed anything. Somewhere between picking Skye up and setting her on the emergency room bed, he'd realized he didn't care anymore. There was someone more important than himself to think about. Right then, it had felt like a switch flipping.

He couldn't tell her that. She'd think it was all because of her, and then she'd feel stuck with him. That was one thing he didn't want. If she did come around and decide to stay, he wanted it to be because she wanted to. Not because she felt sorry for him.

"I guess. Things were happening so fast that I didn't really have a chance to think about it."

The smile disappeared. "I'm so sorry about Robert. I had no idea...and I feel so stupid." She kept her eyes on her fingers as she fidgeted with them.

"You didn't do anything wrong, and you shouldn't

feel that way. It's not stupid to love or trust someone." He took her hand in his. "He's the idiot."

"I guess." She waved him off and yawned. "I'm worn out, and these hormones aren't helping any."

As he went to stand, she grabbed his hand. "You think you could lie down with me for a bit?"

"Whatever you want."

For a second, she held his gaze like she wanted to say something. Then she smiled. "Thanks."

He was so tired he was probably seeing things. It didn't stop his heart from galloping or the wild speculation of what might have run through her mind. As he settled in next to her, he shoved the thoughts away.

All she needed or wanted was comfort. If he could give her that, he would without wondering or plotting what might be the motivation. He'd hold her, care for her, and anything else she wanted while he had the chance. It was way more than he ever thought he'd have. Funny thing, it was all because his grandpa pushed him. Perhaps it was time to revisit all those conversations they'd had about love and life.

CHAPTER 20

W alking through the door of her own home in Caprock Canyon did more for Skye's morale than balloons or flowers could ever do. She'd been afraid they'd keep her after Robert's visit. She wouldn't have argued, but the hospital bed was incredibly uncomfortable and small. At least at home she had a queen-size bed all to herself.

Her family had followed her and Bandit home, allowing her dad and brother to check out her place. They'd stayed for a short visit and then left. Since Skye's chat with her mom, things between them were better than they'd been in years. Of course, there were still little things, but no one was perfect overnight.

Easing down in the recliner, Skye exhaled slowly and lifted the footrest. "I think this is the most comfortable I've been since leaving yesterday morning." Physically, that was. Emotionally and mentally, she was still reeling from Robert's visit.

Finding out he'd asked her dad for a job left her flabbergasted. She'd had no clue he'd ever approached him looking for employment. Robert was a CPA and a partner at his firm. He made plenty of money, so why he'd wanted a job at her parents' construction company made no sense to her.

"Is there anything I can get you?" Bandit asked.

"Not right now."

A knock came from the door, and they exchanged puzzled looks. Then Bandit sighed. "I'll bet the farm it's the Wests."

"It's okay. They can visit." Although she was tired, she appreciated that they cared enough to check on her.

"Are you sure? I don't mind telling them they can come back at another time."

"I'm positive."

Crossing the room to the door, he gave her one last glance as he answered it. "Come on in."

"It's just us," Caroline said as she walked in with Winnie, Bear, Carrie Anne, Gabby, and a few women Skye hadn't met yet. Caroline turned to the others, pointing them out and introducing them. "This is

Pauline, my best friend, and her daughter, Stephanie. Molly is Josiah's wife, and Reagan is Hunter's wife. We left the kids with the men." She winked and laughed.

Skye gave a small wave. "Hi." Then she noticed Gabby and Winnie carrying something. "Uh...is that pie?" She directed the question to Gabby.

"And mushroom risotto," Winnie replied, holding up her small sealed dish. "Extra mushrooms just for you."

"I am a little hungry." She could have been as full as a tick and still eaten it.

Bear shook Bandit's hand. "I'm not staying. Just wanted to see how you two were doing real quick."

"I think we're good." Bandit smiled.

A grin broke out on Bear's face. "All right." He'd never made a big deal about Bandit stuttering. His friend had never even mentioned it. They were friends, flaws and all. "I'll be going, then."

Caroline touched Bandit's shoulder. "Why don't you get some rest? We'll make sure she's taken care of, okay?"

Shaking his head, he replied, "I'm okay."

That wasn't true, and Skye knew it. The small bed at the hospital barely fit her, and he'd spent the entire night next to her. If she wasn't comfortable, neither was he, especially when she was half lying on him the whole time. She probably squished the stuffing out of him. Plus, anytime she commented about something, he was up and getting it for her.

"She's right. You need some rest too." Skye gave him a pointed look. "Go lie down a while. I'm fine."

"I—"

"Go take a nap." Her words came out as firm as she could make them.

Laughing, Bear said, "Better listen to her."

Skye beamed. "Yep."

It was like she'd given him permission to relax. His shoulders sagged, and he yawned. Handing his phone to her, he replied, "I'll leave this with you so you can tell Emilia what's going on, okay? You come get me if you need anything." He made a point to lock gazes with her and then the rest of the visitors.

The second he shut his door, Winnie clasped Bear's arm. "Did you hear him?"

"I did." Bear bowed his head. "I'll see you later, sweetheart. Have fun visiting." He strode to the door and threw one last bye in their direction.

Winnie caught Caroline's gaze. "Isn't it wonderful?"

Tears sprang to her eyes. "I didn't want to say anything, but I'm as tickled as can be." Caroline looked at Skye. "His speech has weighed so heavily on him for so long. I'm just thrilled for him."

Carrie Anne wiped a tear from her cheek. "I've known him forever. I couldn't be happier."

The other women nodded. Gabby's mom, Pauline smiled. "His momma would be beside herself. I so wish she were here."

"Me too," Caroline replied and sat on the couch closest to Skye. "How are *you* doing? Bandit called and we wanted to visit, but we didn't want to overwhelm you. Those hospital rooms are tiny. Doesn't take many people to fill them up."

Skye nodded. "Actually, I appreciate that."

"Uh, before I sit, I'm going to go plate some of this up first." Winnie pointed to the kitchen.

Gabby followed her as the rest of the family parked themselves.

Molly sat forward. "Have you heard from Emilia yet?"

"No, not yet." Skye desperately wanted her to call and soon. There were so many questions and zero answers.

"She's the absolute best." Molly then went on to tell Skye about what had happened with her. It wasn't the same thing that was happening to Skye, but it wasn't any less scary. At least Skye's mom didn't want to take her baby.

Winnie returned from the kitchen carrying a plate of risotto with chunks of mushroom everywhere. Skye's mouth watered as she inhaled the earthy smell of the mushrooms steeped in beef broth. "Oh, this…" She scooped up a spoonful and melted as the flavors exploded in her mouth. "So, so good."

Laughing, Gabby nodded. "That's how I am every time I eat that. Just save room for pie."

"Not a problem." Skye chuckled and took another bite.

From there, the conversation flowed like Skye had been a member of the family for years. It amazed her how easily they accepted people into their fold. Although, now that she'd made peace with her mom, her family had wrapped around Bandit, too, like he wasn't going anywhere after their year was up.

It was sweet, but they didn't have all the information. She'd left out the part where Robert had threatened Bandit. His claim that he could expose their arrangement to the court didn't scare her. She could handle that. It was the ominous way he spoke about Bandit being in an accident that chilled her, and she wasn't sure what was worse, that he'd voiced it or that he could threaten such a thing. It put a spotlight on her choices. How could she have married a man like that?

A small part of her wondered if she'd made the right choice by keeping the information from Bandit and her family. In the end, Skye had reasoned that until Emilia called, all it would do was worry people. With the scare that just happened, it seemed like just another thing to cause stress.

If the private investigator called while she was alone, it would give Skye a chance to tell Emilia about the veiled threat. If the woman was as professional as Skye was led to believe, she'd never tell Bandit about their conversation. She just hoped the call didn't happen while his family was still visiting. It wasn't something she wanted his family to know either. At least until she knew if he could actually follow through on it. She didn't want them worrying over nothing.

A couple of hours later, Skye was thanking them for the food and the fun visit as they left. Bandit had commented more than once that his family was huge and close-knit, but she'd compared it to her own family. It was large and somewhat close. As in they knew when someone was getting married, when a cousin was having a quinceañera, or there was a death. The big details. Major events.

What made this family stand out was the small details. When Skye spoke, they weren't half listening. They concentrated on what she was saying. Asking questions. Offering ideas or counsel. It was so different how active they were in each other's lives.

At the last goodbye, the door shut, and Skye rested her head against the back of the chair. As much as she enjoyed talking, it was nice to just sit there in the peace and quiet.

It lasted all of a few minutes, when Bandit's phone lit up. She jerked her head up and quickly answered, hoping he hadn't heard it. "Hello?"

"Hi, this is Emilia Sanger. May I speak to Bandit Ochoa?" The voice on the other line was both feminine and firm. It fit with the line of work she was in.

"This is Skye...Ochoa." That was the first time she'd referred to herself as belonging to Bandit. A tiny thrill raced down her spine. It felt pretty good to claim him.

"Oh, hi. I think you are the one I am looking for anyway. Josiah said you needed help?"

"That's me." Skye looked over her shoulder in the direction of Bandit's room. She stood and walked to the kitchen, hoping the conversation didn't wake him up.

"Start from the beginning. Leave nothing out. Even things you might not think matter. Okay?"

Taking a deep breath, Skye sat at the table and started with how and where she'd met Robert. Businesses in the area met every other week at different locations to network with each other. From hotel owners to plumbing companies, from locally-owned to national chains to self-employed entrepreneurs, typically catered by a restaurant in the area.

That night, Robert's firm had hosted it at their office. They'd struck up a conversation and exchanged numbers, and later she'd found out he'd only done that so he could ask her out. She thought it was sweet. Their first date was incredible, and by the third, they were an item. He showered her with chocolates and flowers for the first few months.

Gradually, it changed, and the chocolates and flowers stopped, but that's what happened with relationships. Couples got comfortable with each other. That's just how it worked, or that's how she thought they worked.

As she relayed the details, what she found most enlightening were the details she'd glossed over from the beginning. How the first date was him talking nonstop about himself. The way he'd always say something about how she dressed. Her hair. Her makeup.

Things she'd ignored because of the grand gestures, like somehow that made up for the rest of it.

"His business trips went from every other month to monthly to bi-weekly. He said it was because the firm had government clients and he had to travel to give demonstrations to the different public entities." She stood and walked to the counter where the aluminum-covered pie beckoned her.

"Do you know where he was going?" asked Emilia.

Skye fished a dish out of the cupboard along with a knife out of the silverware drawer. "I didn't really ask. He said it was work, and I had no reason to question it."

"I see." Her voice sounded distant. The kind when a person was taking notes. "And during all this is when he asked you to marry him?"

Sandwiching the phone between her ear and shoulder, she cut herself a slice of pie. "About six months after we started dating, so in general, yes. We had a short engagement. Three months."

"That is short."

Yeah, no kidding. That was one of the reasons she questioned herself with Bandit. They'd known each other for even less time. "I was in love." She set the knife down as her thoughts traveled back in time. Was she in love? She turned sideways, leaning her hip against the counter. "I thought I was in love."

"I've been there." Emilia laughed. "Keep going."

Skye picked up her plate and waddled back to the table. Between slow bites, she told of their engagement, the months leading up to their marriage, and the day she received the divorce papers. Then she told Emilia about the hospital visit, making sure to note the threat and the look on Robert's face as he leveled it. She made sure to tell her she didn't want Bandit to know about that part.

"All right. Will you be available if I have questions?"

"Absolutely," Skye replied and gave Emilia her own number as well. "I'll do whatever I need to do."

Emilia cleared her throat. "I don't know how long it will take, but you and Bandit might want to stick close to home. Unless it's an emergency. When I find something, I'll let you know."

"Thank you."

They ended the call, and Skye finished off the last few pie bites. Once the dishes were washed, she strolled out of the kitchen to her room, stopping a moment at Bandit's door. After spending the last few weeks with him, she felt lonely when he wasn't around. Before the temptation grew too strong, she shuffled into her bedroom and shut the door.

The stroll down memory lane of her relationship was hard. Even when she thought it was great, it wasn't. For the life of her, she couldn't pin down why she'd allowed herself to endure how Robert treated her. Her mom's criticism had come from a place of concern. Granted, it didn't feel that way to Skye, and the words hurt just the same. But it was different.

Robert was mean-spirited. In just a few months, he had her doubting everything about herself. Enough to the point where she thought she deserved to be treated horribly. That wasn't okay. It was never okay.

Somehow, she'd allowed herself to become dependent on him. But never again. No matter who it was, there would be no next time for that. If nothing else, she owed it to her baby to teach them how they should expect to be treated.

Never again would she allow anyone to walk all over her. She'd keep her head on her shoulders and her standards high. It was a pledge she'd keep. If there was ever another significant other, he'd reach the bar she set or she'd send him packing.

CHAPTER 21

"Bandit!"

Bear's voice cut through Bandit's thoughts, and he urged his horse into a run just before being bulldozed by a bull. To say his head wasn't in his work was an understatement, but that sentiment could've been applied to the last three weeks.

Stopping his horse next to Bandit's, Bear tapped him on the arm. "You okay?"

No, but there was nothing his friend could do about it. After Skye's visit with Robert, things between her and Bandit were different. Not bad, but not great either. He'd ask if things were okay, and she'd assure him they were. Her actions, though, told a different story. She seemed more distant now than she had after she'd kissed him that day after their nap.

He attributed part of it to the fact that Emilia hadn't called with any news. She'd checked in once to say she was working on it. That helped a little, but the lack of anything substantial was disappointing. The woman was thorough, so he'd expected it to take some time, just not as long as it had.

Shrugging, Bandit shook his head. "Naw, I'm all right."

"Is that the same kind of 'all right' as when I said I didn't want a relationship, or the kind of 'all right' as when I was running from Winnie? Because neither of those two was all that *all right*."

Leave it to Bear to speak plainly. "I don't know. I think this thing with her ex-husband shook her up. We haven't heard from Emilia yet, and the man threatened to take her to court for custody. I suspect that wears on a mind, especially a momma's mind."

"I'd reckon so too." Bear looked off into the distance. The slate-gray morning hid any signs that the sun might be hovering over them, making the stretching silence match the mood.

"You know," Bear said, his voice softer than typical for him. "When I was running from Winnie, I thought my feet couldn't pound the pavement hard enough. I knew in my soul that she was the one I wanted, but I held on to my past like a prisoner holding the bars to his cage when the door next to him is wide open."

Bandit bowed his head, offering a small nod in acknowledgment of Bear's words.

"The door is open, my friend. I'm not saying you need to rush anything, but time is the enemy. Every day that slips by is one less you've got." He cleared his throat. "I will never have enough time to show Winnie how much I love her, and those minutes I wasted, I can never get back."

Lifting his head, Bandit locked gazes with Bear. "This is a little different."

"Everyone says that. In the end, it really isn't. Time ticks the same for all of us." He took a deep breath and smiled. "That said, Winnie is supposed to be calling Skye about having dinner tonight. She said the last time they talked, Skye didn't sound right. Winnie's hoping a little food and fellowship will help."

"If Winnie can convince Skye to leave the house, I think it'd be good for her. Every time I've tried, she's declined. Her doctor appointments are the only thing she'll leave home for."

Bear rested his hands on his saddle horn. "Makes me wonder if something else didn't happen when that Robert fella talked to her."

With a nod, Bandit agreed. He'd thought of that

too, but she hadn't kept anything from him so far. He had no reason to think she'd start now. There wasn't anything that guy could do to Bandit.

He'd also considered nesting. One night, sleepless as he'd ever been, he'd decided to look up some pregnancy articles. Most all of them said a woman went through a period of excessive cleaning and making sure everything was in its proper place. In the midst of that, Skye had plenty of things on her mind, and her orbit didn't revolve around Bandit.

A gale of wind knocked the clouds enough that the sun was able to peek through, warning Bandit it was past time to go home. While Skye was a little distant, she didn't like him being late. Her switch between hot and cold was just part of the hormones she was dealing with, so he'd done his best not to add to her stress.

"I need to get home. I'll see you tonight." Bandit smiled.

Bear tipped his hat and pushed his horse into a trot while Bandit headed off in the opposite direction. Once he had his horse taken care of, he strode to the house. The warmth was a welcomed sensation, even if it did make his skin tingle as it thawed.

The sound of crying pricked his ears, and he shucked off his coat, not caring if it hit the coat hook or the floor, and he didn't look back as he went in search of the source of the waterworks. When he reached Skye's room, he tapped on the door. "Hey, you okay?"

A couple of sniffles. "Yes." Another sniffle. "No." Then hiccups as the crying started again. "I don't know." The words squeaked out.

Taking a chance, he pushed the door open a little while keeping his gaze pinned to the floor just in case. "That doesn't sound like nothing's wrong."

"I'm decent," she grumbled, but it didn't sound specifically aimed at him.

He lifted his gaze to her. "All right. Want to tell me what's got you so upset?"

She pinched the bridge of her nose and began to pace the length of her bed. "I keep dropping everything I pick up. I spilled my sugar and my coffee on my favorite pajamas, so I changed my clothes. Then while I was frying eggs, grease popped on me and I had to change into this stupid nightgown because it's the only thing that seems to fit me now."

"Okay." That seemed about the safest answer he could give.

"Then Winnie called and invited us to dinner." She stopped pacing and waved her hand down her body. "Do I look like I should be seen in public? I'm as big as a whale, and you'd think I'd be used to it, but I went to try on a dress I thought for sure I could wear that fit."

This time he didn't even dare a word. He wasn't much of a dater, but he knew what danger sounded like. He just nodded.

"It fit." She huffed. "Of course! The one dress that fits and I don't have any leggings to match. Nothing." The speed with which she spoke seemed to increase. "I can't shave my legs. I can't even see them. And my toes? Who knows what those look like? I'm just…" Her lips and chin trembled. "I'm just a big fat hairy cow." She wailed again and collapsed onto the bed, dissolving into a torrent of tears.

He crossed the room and squatted in front of her. "Darlin', it's okay. Winnie is family. I don't think she'll be looking at your legs, but you just hold on." He tipped her chin up, and she sniffled. "I'll be right back."

With a little nod, she snatched a handful of tissues from the box on her nightstand. "Okay."

He straightened and left her room to gather a few supplies. With a bowl of warm water, a razor, a towel, and a table chair, he returned and set the chair in front of her. "Let me see your legs."

Her eyes widened, and she pulled them in as much as she could, yanking her nightgown over them. "You can't see me like that! I've got forests."

Chuckling, he motioned with his hand for her leg. "Good thing I'm a lumberjack." He winked.

"But…"

"Sweetheart, let me see your legs."

She held his gaze a few moments and slowly unfurled her legs. "They're awful."

Without a word, he lathered up her right leg first and shaved it, and then he started on the left. While he worked, his mind walked to a memory of his mom before she passed away. It had been so long since he'd thought about taking care of her while she was sick.

"My momma got really sick before she died. She wanted to go to church one Sunday, but she'd get dizzy after standing too long. Shaving her legs was just too hard, and she wouldn't wear pants. That wasn't how she was taught to go to church." He laughed. "So, I said, 'Momma, do you really want to go to church?' And she said, 'I sure would like to, but I can't go looking like this. I guess I'll just stay home.'"

That memory may as well have been playing in color right in front of him with as clear as it was. Man, he loved her. "So, I shaved her legs and then I painted her toes."

Using a pair of nail clippers, he quickly took care of her toenails. Once finished, he snagged a polish bottle and painted her toes. He grunted a laugh as he ran the brush over one of Skye's nails. "You should have seen her that day. Boy, she was so proud of her toes. All through the service, I caught her wiggling her toes as she looked at them."

He set the bottle and clippers back where he'd gotten them and picked up the bowl and razor. Bracing his hand on the chair back, he said, "I didn't know it at the time, but that was the last Sunday I would have the privilege of taking her to church." With a sigh, he picked up the chair. "If I could have her back, I'd shave her legs and paint her toenails every day."

Before he could take a step, Skye stood, cupped his cheek, and kissed him. Not like the blazing kisses they'd shared before. It was tender and sweet. More like taffy than cinnamon dots. While he wouldn't knock those hot kisses, this one meant more to him.

"Thank you. I…" She chewed her bottom lip. "Just thank you."

Catching her gaze, he replied, "My pleasure."

The door quietly closed behind him as he left so she could get ready. Bear was right. Every day he waited was one less kiss he'd get to give her. One less chance to hold her. One less *I love you* he'd get to say. He didn't want to waste his minutes, but he also didn't want to prey on a pregnant woman whose body chemistry was in turmoil. He'd just witnessed firsthand how that worked.

No, he'd wait long enough that he felt right telling her he loved her. Until then, he'd show it. That would speak a heap louder than anything he could say anyway.

CHAPTER 22

Good food and better fellowship tipped Skye's chaotic mind and heart into a better place than it had been in days. Well, more like since her hospital stay, which was three weeks ago. Winnie's invitation had done wonders for Skye's emotional upheaval. She hadn't expected most of the West family to be in attendance, but that had made the meal all the better.

Molly was a hoot. She shared a lot of characteristics with Skye, like blurting out what she was thinking. Listening to her and Josiah speak in movie lines and music quotes had Skye gut-bust laughing more than once.

Then Reagan's Chantilly cake was a win for the

finish. She'd been sweet to use almond extract instead of brandy. It was delicious too. So moist and flavorful with berries in it. It melted in Skye's mouth, but that seemed par for the course with the cooks in the West family.

Standing on the back porch, she leaned against the railing and ran her hand over her huge belly. It had gotten a little too warm for her inside. She normally ran hot anyway, and pregnancy only seemed to ramp that up. Her head was sweating by the time she'd stolen away into the December night air.

The whole evening was an excellent distraction from her thoughts about Bandit. In the weeks waiting for Emilia to call with information, Robert's threat had Skye's imagination working nonstop. From car accidents to full-on hitmen, the scenarios had run the gambit. Each time they'd ended with Skye losing Bandit. Her hormones didn't help either. She wanted Bandit close and at arm's length at the same time. No doubt the poor man wondered about her sanity. She was right there with him.

At the sound of the doorknob jiggling, Skye furiously wiped tears off her face with her hands. She cleared her throat and smiled as Winnie came into view. "Hey."

"Aren't you freezing by now?" Winnie gripped her unzipped coat and yanked it closed.

"No. I think I'm just now starting to cool off."

"Is this what I have to look forward to?" Winnie laughed.

"Doubtful." Skye scrunched up her nose. "You're the kind of pregnant woman who is cute all through her pregnancy."

Rolling her eyes, Winnie replied, "Whatever, you goofball."

Skye pushed off the railing and sat in one of the rocking chairs. "I'm serious. You're the chick standing in the middle of a cotton field looking like a model while I'm hip-checking the plants as I waddle through the rows."

"Girl, whatever. You look great." Winnie shook her head, taking the empty rocker next to Skye. "You haven't had any more pain, right?"

Physically, no. Mentally and emotionally? Agonizingly so. It was bad enough with all the horrible thoughts swimming in her head about harm coming to Bandit. Then…he'd shaved her legs. Her legs. If all the other thoughts didn't have her in an upheaval, that certainly did. She'd felt like an ogre, and she'd expected him to look at her in disgust. Only, he didn't even flinch. Didn't say anything negative or rude. He'd just done it. She'd thrown an all-out temper tantrum, and he'd responded more calmly and kindly than anyone she'd ever met. She'd barely been able to muster the words *thank you* before shutting her door and running to her bathroom to weep a bucket full of tears.

"I've been fine," Skye said. "But I'm going to tell you right now. If those weren't labor pains…" She whistled. "All those labor books…they lie."

With a snort, Winnie crossed her legs. "I guess it's sort of hard to convey blinding agony with words."

"Must be, because…wow." She sighed.

"Have you heard from Emilia?"

"No, and it's getting harder to be patient. I wish I'd known about Robert asking for a job from my dad. I really had no idea."

Winnie nodded. "Yeah, that's weird, especially for a man who's a partner in a CPA firm. I mean, he should be making pretty good money. It's not an overnight thing to become a partner, either. Why would he want to leave that after working so hard to get it?"

Shrugging, Skye replied, "I don't even have a guess." With a long exhale, she forced the stress and tension from her shoulders while gazing up at the sparkly night sky. Wisps of clouds shaped like hands cupped the stars, making them look like loose glitter blown on satin fabric.

"So, want to tell me the other reason why you're out here?" Winnie glanced at Skye. "And don't lie. I know what I saw in there between you and Bandit."

She'd known the question would be coming. As hard as she'd tried to mask it, there wasn't a person at the dinner table who could have missed the weird energy between her and Bandit. One minute, she wanted to drown in his eyes, and the next, she wanted to be sealed in a bubble until the end of their contract to keep herself from making a mistake.

"Come on, Skye. I know you. Just tell me."

"What's to tell?" Not the best response, but if she spoke the words, it would make them real. Was she ready for real? "We have a contract."

"Oh, please. I had a contract too. Bear West showed up at that restaurant, and that was all she wrote. Attractive, sweet, and thoughtful. I thought I could walk away too."

"It's different." Skye kept her focus on the dark horizon in front of her. If she didn't, she'd be a blubbering idiot. "I haven't even known him that long."

"I didn't know Bear that long either." Shrugging, Winnie sighed. "But what do I know. I'm sure Bandit won't have any trouble finding someone to love when you move on."

Skye jerked her gaze to Winnie. Bandit finding someone…else? "What?" Head wise, she knew that was true, but her heart was bucking at the thought.

Stone-faced, Winnie leaned back in the rocking chair. "You heard me. With that smile of his and his kind nature, he'll have women lining up to take your place."

"You're just trying to make me jealous."

"Jealous? I thought you were just friends with him." Winnie smiled. "Just think. This time next year… Bandit showing off his new girlfriend, them kissing and holding each other. It'll be so cute. Probably for the best anyway. I mean, I doubt you'd be happy with him."

Skye turned in her seat and faced Winnie. "I'd be perfectly happy with him. He's beyond just kind and generous. He goes out of his way to make people happy. Me happy. I was acting like a she-beast today, and what does he do? Shaves my legs and paints my toenails because I didn't have any leggings to go with this dress."

"But that doesn't matter. You have a contract."

"Just because we have a contract doesn't mean it has to end." The second it was out of her mouth, Skye covered her face with her hands. "Shut it, you redheaded troublemaker."

One giggle popped out and then another before Winnie was hysterically laughing. "Yes, yes, I am."

Skye peeked through her fingers and then dropped her hands to her lap. "I made so many mistakes with Robert. I know Bandit is different in every way, but I can't shake that fear. And then I have this baby that isn't Bandit's. He's kind enough to offer to raise a child who isn't his, but how will I know he means it? What if I'm making another mistake?"

"Do you really want to live life that way? Driven by the fear of making mistakes? What if staying with Bandit is the best decision of your life? Of your child's life? No relationship is perfect. Bear and I have our moments, but that doesn't mean I made a mistake. It means that I love him enough to walk through things with him, loving him even more on the other side."

"There's more to it, and you know it."

"Those are excuses. You're using Robert like a crutch to keep yourself from getting hurt again."

Okay, maybe there was a grain of truth to that. Getting the divorce papers in the mail had crushed her. At the time, she'd thought she'd found the love of her life and that she'd be spending the rest of her life with him. Since then, she'd become cognizant that her relationship wasn't as great as she tried to talk herself into thinking. It had been horrible, really. She'd taken more abuse than she was comfortable to admit.

All of that could be true, but it didn't change that she was a walking emotional tinderbox. Setting her elbow on the chair arm, Skye palmed her forehead. "I'm pregnant. How do I know if what I'm feeling is even true?"

"How does the thought of Bandit making out with other women and possibly marrying one of them make you feel?"

Skye lifted her head, her left eye involuntarily twitching and her stomach souring. "Murderous rage and a healthy fear of prison."

Winnie covered her mouth as she laughed. "You're a mess. You know that, right?"

Suddenly, a weird pop ran through her body like a tremor. She sucked in a sharp breath and froze. "I think my water just broke."

"What?" Winnie scoffed. "If you wanted out of the conversation, you could have just said so."

"No, really. I think it just broke. Either that or I've lost all ability to not pee myself. Which is a real possibility. Sneezing is more like Russian roulette lately." The tiny little aches she'd experienced throughout the evening intensified to cut through her, and she winced. "Yeah, I need to go to the hospital."

She'd thought they were just more Braxton Hicks contractions, but maybe they'd been more. She was still four weeks from her due date, but the doctor had told her any time after thirty-six weeks was fair game.

Winnie startled and jumped up. "Uh...stay there, and I'll get help."

"I'll be here." She shifted in the chair and held the underside of her stomach.

The beginning stages of labor didn't take her mind off Bandit for long. She'd been physically ill picturing him with another woman. And lip-locking one of them? That didn't sit well at all.

Her friend was right, though. She'd been using her relationship with Robert as an easy way out. Truthfully, the same could be said about the baby. She'd used her pregnancy hormones like bubble wrap to keep herself from getting hurt.

Since the moment Bandit walked into her life, he'd made her heart skip a beat. Beyond generous and kind, he backed up his sweet words with actions. She'd made a mistake with her last relationship because she'd settled for what she thought she deserved.

Hormones or not...she loved Bandit. Whether their relationship was three days or three hundred years, she couldn't picture wanting to stand next to anyone but him.

Another contraction hit, and she gripped the chair arms. Of course, she'd have her stroke of brilliance as she went into labor. Her poor timing was at least predictable.

CHAPTER 23

Straining through a contraction, Skye's grip on Bandit's hand was nearly bone-crushing. He'd seen it in the movies and thought the fellas were a little wimpy, but now that he was experiencing it, he could understand shedding a few tears.

The nurse finished checking Skye and typed on the iPad she was carrying. "Not super long now."

"What's that mean? 'Not super long'?" asked Skye in a rush as the contraction waned.

"A few more hours."

Skye's jaw dropped. "You mean it gets worse?"

The nurse worked to keep a smile off her face. "They'll get more intense the closer they get."

Dropping her head back against the pillow, Skye groaned. She would be in the percentage of pregnant women to get an epidural and have it not work. "There has to be an easier way to do this."

Winnie snickered. "I hope you figure it out before it's my turn."

"I'll be back in to check on you in a little while." The nurse turned and walked out of the room.

The Wests had followed them to Amarillo and arrived along with Skye's family shortly after Bandit, Skye, and Winnie made it to the hospital. Her family, with Bear and Caroline, had gone downstairs to grab a few drinks while the nurse had stopped in to look at Skye. Her sister's plan to fly in a week later had been changed, and she'd taken the first flight out of Houston.

Winnie stood. "I think I'm going to go walk around a little. Is there anything I can get you? A pillow or something?"

Skye shook her head. "No." It came out whiny.

"All right. I'll see you in a minute."

Once she was gone, Skye exhaled heavily. "I knew it would hurt worse than those Braxton Hicks, but no one could have ever prepared me for this."

Bandit extracted his hand from hers and flexed it. Taking the rag from the bowl of water, he wrung it out and wiped her face. "You are one tough mama."

She rolled her eyes. "I am not."

"Yes, you are." He could say that with confidence. "You're being a trouper."

"I think this kid is mad and doing his best to claw my insides raw."

He dropped the rag in the bowl and shifted from his chair to sit beside her. "You think it's a boy?"

"Did I say he?"

"Yeah," he said, nodding. "Boy or girl, as long as they're healthy. That's all that matters."

Another contraction hit, and Skye let out a deep guttural noise as the pain ripped through her body. "I need to talk to you."

"We can talk once the baby is here."

"No." She strained out the word as she tensed. "Now."

"I think you've got other things to concentrate on."

"Oh, oh, oh." She grabbed her stomach and grunted. "I can't get comfortable." Leaning up on one elbow, she turned on her side. "My back is killing me."

On a television show Bandit remembered watching a long time ago, a man sat behind a woman who was giving birth. It seemed to help. "How about I sit behind you and you lean against me?"

The contraction peaked, knocking the wind from her for a second, then she said, "I think I'm willing to try anything."

After situating himself behind her, she wilted against him with a long sigh. "Better. Thank you."

He combed his fingers through her hair. "As long as it helps."

"It does."

As the minutes ticked by, the longer the silence seemed to stretch, to the point where he wondered if she'd fallen asleep.

"Bandit, could we talk a minute?" She craned her neck to look at him.

"Is everything okay? Need me to move?"

"Everything's okay. I just—" Her phone ringing cut her off midsentence. He grabbed it from the nightstand and handed it to her. "Emilia?" she answered. "Sure."

The phone lit up again, and Skye answered the video call. Emilia's eyes widened. "Are you in the hospital?"

"Yeah."

"I thought you were due in January."

Skye shrugged. "I'm early."

Emilia's jaw hung open a minute. "I want to say I'll call back, but I think you want this information."

Bandit noted the undecorated wood paneling behind Emilia and a lack of pictures. At first it struck him as odd, but when he considered what she did for a living, it made sense. Keeping a separation line between her work and her family was smart.

"Please." She grunted a laugh. "I'm told it'll be a few hours."

"Then let's get started." Emilia opened a file folder and then looked at the camera. "So, Robert Faulks." She took a deep breath. "Is not Robert Faulks. His name is Robert Harris, and he's not a CPA."

"What?" The question rushed out. "Not a CPA?"

"No. He's a divorced father of three. Those business trips he was taking was him going back home to his kids in Delaware because he shares custody with his ex-wife."

Skye let out a small whimper. "He said he was single. That he'd never been married. He lied about all of it?"

Bandit's already low opinion of the man sank a little lower. He'd lied to Skye about everything on top of the way he'd treated her. This certainly wouldn't help her confidence, and he couldn't even blame her.

"Well, he was working at the CPA office, but as a janitor. When I called them about the business meeting they'd held, they had no idea what I was talking about. Needless to say, they were rather unhappy to find out that he'd not only lied about his true employment but that he'd also volunteered their office to host the meeting."

Bandit scoffed. How could those fellows have that sort of office and not know her ex had done something like that? "How did they not know what happened?"

Emilia flipped a page in the file. "Each year they take the office and their families on a cruise. Those who were working there the year prior. By the time they returned, nothing looked out of place. Typically, those types of meetings cost as well, and they didn't get a bill. Once I dug into it, Robert had intercepted it before they returned and paid it."

"But…I met him there. He…" She sucked in a sharp breath as her hands covered her mouth. "He always met me outside. Anytime I asked to meet his partners, he'd say they were somewhere else or too busy."

"Not surprising. I also found out he's done this before. At the time, he wasn't married, but he'd dated two women at the same time, each in different states. Until I spoke to them, they had no idea. He just broke it off one day."

Bandit shook his head and cursed under his breath. "What a worthless man. Does his ex-wife know?"

"I haven't spoken to her yet. I wanted to speak to you first."

Closing her eyes, Skye huffed. "How stupid could I be?"

Shaking her head, Emilia said, "No, you weren't stupid at all. The guy was good at covering his tracks. I've been a PI for a long time, and I had to dig. These sorts of things hardly ever take me as long as this one did. At one point, I wondered if I was going to come back empty-handed."

"But..."

"Skye, really. He's not just a run-of-the-mill con man. He keeps his activities low-key, and if he thinks he's about to get caught, he cuts ties and runs. I'm a little surprised he visited you in the hospital."

"Lousy two-timing, two-faced jerk!"

Bandit tilted his head. "Why did he visit Skye? You would think he would've stayed gone."

Emilia held up her finger. "This is where it gets really interesting." She smiled akin to a cat catching a mouse. "Before landing in Amarillo, Robert was passing himself off as a real estate agent and selling land he didn't own. His mistake was finding a guy who wasn't what you'd call...reputable. When he found out Robert conned him, he demanded his money back."

"So he wanted to skim off her parents to pay that guy back?" Bandit asked.

"Yep, that's exactly what he was planning." She

paused, looking from Skye to Bandit and back again. Bandit wasn't always the sharpest crayon, but he knew what a secret looked like. "I don't think you have to worry about him trying anything."

Skye tensed and grunted as her phone dropped to the bed. Her fingernails dug through Bandit's jeans, nearly making him yelp.

"Thanks, Emilia," he said.

"I'll let the police know to give you a few days before contacting you for a statement."

By the time Bandit had Skye's phone back on the nightstand, her contraction subsided. If he didn't need stitches, he'd consider himself lucky. He grabbed the rag, wrung it out, and wiped her forehead. "That one seemed a little longer than the others."

"They all seem to last forever to me."

"Mind telling me what that look was that Emilia gave you?"

"Um…" Skye fidgeted with her hands. "Robert threatened to hurt you. Just not outright. More like hinting that you could have an accident or something. I'd just had a scare, and I didn't want anyone to worry over something that. Apparently, no one needed to be concerned about it."

"I wish you'd told me. You don't need to carry concerns like that on your own anymore." He placed his hands on her shoulders. "I wish you'd trusted me." He'd worked hard to earn her trust. Granted, their relationship was relatively new, but he'd done everything he could to show her he was different. That she could rely on him.

Twisting a little in the bed to face him, she replied, "You've done so much for me. I've done hardly anything for you, at least nothing hard."

"I wouldn't say that..." He smiled. "You married me and—"

"All the things you did for me were huge. The bedroom and bathroom and all the little things. Most of them were permanent, and all I did was marry you." Her eyes widened as his face fell. His heart breaking must have shown in his eyes. "Bandit—"

The hospital door swished open, and Winnie, Bear, Caroline, and Skye's family walked in laughing. "Hey, you two." Her mom smiled.

Shooting his best fake smile, Bandit extricated himself from his position behind Skye and stood. "I think I'm going to let you all visit. My legs need some stretching."

He needed a second to put himself back together. While he'd been picturing forever, she'd been seeing things as temporary. His heart wasn't just broken; it was crushed. How was he going to love her...love his baby, and then watch her leave at the end of the year?

"Bandit…"

"I'll see you in a few minutes." He caught Winnie's gaze and then quickly pinned it to the floor. "If something happens, call and I'll be here."

He strode out of the room, nearly breaking into a run to catch the elevator without a care whether it was going up or down. He plastered himself in one of the corners, and his eyes slid shut at the ache tearing through him. He still had ten and a half months with Skye…and his heart was already in shreds. What on earth was he going to do now?

CHAPTER 24

Skye pinched her lips together and crossed her arms over her chest. "Bear, go get Bandit and drag him back here if you have to."

"Uh…"

Winnie nodded furiously. "Just do what she says. It's good practice for when I go into labor."

As he left, another contraction hit Skye, and she flopped back, balling her fists in the bedsheets. "Holy whoa." She pointed to the door. "Dad, Andy. Out!" One of the only perks of labor she liked was the way people listened. She grunted through the pain and took a breath as it eased.

"Bear needs to get Bandit back here," she said when she could talk.

"What happened?" her mom asked.

"I was trying to tell him I love him, but it came out wrong." She rolled her eyes. "I said all I'd done was little things. Non-permanent stuff. He took it that I meant our marriage. He didn't say it in those words, but I saw the look in his eyes."

Winnie's eyebrows slowly lifted. "I so knew it."

"Fine. So, I am." She crossed her arms over her chest again, using her stomach as a table.

Her mom took Skye's hand. "He's a good man. Your dad, Andy, and Jen like him too. I know Robert was awful—"

Skye held up her hand. "He was, and without him, I wouldn't have Bandit. I really—" A spider web of pain wrapped around her, and she groaned. What she really wanted was for Bandit to return. Not only was it more comfortable to lean on him, but she also felt better when he was around.

The longer he was gone, the more her heart ached, much worse than the contractions that were coming almost constantly now. What if she'd pushed him far enough this time that he wouldn't listen? Or trust her, which she couldn't blame him. She'd been the one all over the place with one minute being happy and the next moody.

A knock came from the door, and the nurse from earlier peeked her head in. "Just checking in." She smiled and pushed the rest of the way into the room. "How are we doing?"

"I think—" Skye pushed up on her hands, bracing herself with one while she clutched her stomach with the other. Everything she read said these things lasted at most ninety seconds. They'd never convince her of that, ever. It felt more like an eternity. As the pain subsided, she flopped back. "I think they're getting closer."

The snap of gloves made her cringe. This part of being a woman had never been on her list of awesome things to start with, and now, it was worse.

As the nurse finished her exam, she pulled off her gloves and dumped them in a biohazard bucket. "You've definitely progressed. The—"

An involuntary need to push hit, and whatever the nurse was about to say was lost on Skye. The intensity of the contractions seemed to be getting worse too. Panting, she lay back and palmed her forehead. "I really just want Bandit."

"I'm here." His voice had never been more soothing. He crossed the room and stopped. "How can I help?"

"Don't leave again." She was pathetic, but she didn't care. Just having him in the room was a boost for her morale.

He sat beside her. "I won't leave again. You have my word."

She wrapped her arms around his neck. "I'm sorry."

"Nothing to be sorry for," he replied as he pulled her to him. "That was all on me." He glanced over his shoulder. "Would you ladies mind if I talked to Skye in private a moment?"

"Not at all." Her mom grinned and hooked her arm in Winnie's.

Was this it? The part where he told her she was too difficult? That the best he could muster was friendship? Whatever it was he wanted to say wouldn't change how she felt about him, and she'd tell him as much.

CHAPTER 25

Bandit waited until the door clicked shut and leaned back. "I'm sorry I took off. I shouldn't have done that."

Bear didn't have to chew hard to hit it home that Bandit was stupid. Skye was in the hospital about to give birth, and he was making it about himself? It was selfish and self-centered. She'd already put up with a man like that, and she didn't need it from him.

"You came back. That's what matters."

"No, I shouldn't have left. It was a cowardly thing to do." He rubbed his hands up and down her arms. "Once we get back home and settled, I'd like to talk if we can. That is, when you're up to it."

Her gaze locked with his, and they may as well have been on a deserted island. Taking his face in her hands, she touched her lips to his. "I wasn't saying that I wanted our marriage to be temporary. I was trying to say that…meeting you was the best thing to happen to me."

"I think you got that twisted around."

She pinched his lips together with her fingers. "Hush. I'm dealing with contractions, and they're getting closer together. I've got a time problem and words I need to say." Her hand slid to his cheek.

He nodded.

Just then another one hit, and she gritted her teeth while it pulsed through her body. Now she wished she'd taken those birth classes, but at the time, she thought they were goofy. Like, who doesn't know to breathe? Apparently, people in pain, as she was currently realizing.

She held on to him to steady herself. "Okay, I'm going to try to get this all out before the next one." A chuckle popped out. "To make it short and sweet, I'm in love with you."

"Oh." It was the best word he had. He'd expected… well, he wasn't sure. Maybe a good thump for leaving her in the first place, but not that she loved him.

"It just came out wrong."

He chuckled. If that wasn't a sign of meeting his

soul mate, he didn't know what was. "Seems we had the same idea."

"What?" She tilted her head.

"Nothing I've done comes close to measuring how much I love you. I don't want anyone but you." He held her gaze. "You remember that wager we had? I needed time to think on it?

She tilted her head as she smiled. "Yeah."

"Can we be married for real, and we can set that contract on fire?"

"I'd love to." As she nodded, a smile lifted her lips, and then she grimaced, her hands balling in his shirt. "I'd say let's kiss on it, but I'm not sure that's safe right now." She grunted, pressing her forehead into his shoulder.

"I think I should get the nurse."

She shot him a combination of a grin and a grimace. "I think so too."

Once Bandit called in the nurse, everything went faster than he'd expected. He'd heard the term sensory overload, but that was as close to an accurate description as he could get. One minute, Skye was pushing like the doctor told her to, and the next, the cry of a screaming infant filled the room.

With the baby boy measured, weighed, and

cleaned, he was handed to Skye. Tears rolled down her cheeks. "Isn't he beautiful?" She looked up at Bandit.

He slipped his finger into one of the baby's hands. "He sure is." He was, too. Just as perfect a baby as Bandit had ever seen. "You never told me what you wanted to name him."

She cast her gaze to their son. "I was trying not to think about it since I didn't want to know if it was a boy or girl. I didn't want to get attached to a name. What do you think?"

"We could name him after your father." Bandit smiled.

"Or your grandpa, Mauricio."

"I'd be fine with either." Mike was a good man, and his grandpa was the reason Bandit was sitting next to Skye.

"Want to hold him?"

Something so tiny? "Uh…"

When she held him out to Bandit, he took the baby and cradled him in his arms. At that moment, blood didn't matter a lick to him. This baby was his, and he never realized he could love someone as fiercely as he loved this baby boy.

"He's so perfect—" He cut the sentence short as his voice broke.

She caught her bottom lip in her teeth. "How about

Christopher Michael Ochoa? I can't think of two better men."

As if he wasn't choked up enough. Naming the baby after him? "That's a big honor." More than he could ever have hoped for. He'd known from the beginning that he wanted the baby, but carrying his name…it was a gift. "I'm more than okay with that."

The door to the room opened, and Jen bounced in. "I missed it. I'm so sorry."

Skye shrugged. "You're here now."

The rest of their family piled in. Shortly after the baby was born, they'd quietly left to give Skye and Bandit a moment. He was surprised they lasted as long as they did. Her mom was nearly falling over herself to hold the baby.

Jen crossed the room and stopped next to Bandit. "He has Skye's eyes."

"And his mom's cheeks." Bandit winked.

"What name did you decide on?" asked their mom.

Beaming, Skye said, "Christopher Michael Ochoa."

"Michael?" her dad said just above a whisper. "After me?"

"Oh, honey." Doreen hugged his bicep. "That's a great name."

Bandit stood and handed Mike his grandson. The

man looked down at the baby and back up to Skye. "Sweetheart, he's just…"

Caroline sniffed. "Perfect. Just absolutely perfect." She hugged Bandit. "Oh, sweetie, your momma would be so tickled and proud of you." She wiped at her eyes. "You do know this is my grandson, right?"

Bear and Winnie huddled around Mike. "Oh my gosh, Skye. He's so cute," Winnie said.

"He sure is." Bear stopped short of touching him. "If this is even a taste of what it'll be like when we have our baby…wow." He stuck his hand out and shook Bandit's.

Bandit took a deep breath and glanced heavenward. He wasn't sure who he needed to thank most for what he'd been given. All he knew was he'd never felt more blessed in his life. He had a woman he loved, a son he would cherish as long as he had breath, and a family he'd lay his life down for.

This. What he had right then was worth everything in the world to him.

EPILOGUE

Christmas day...

Two weeks, Skye thought as she looked down at the bundle in her arms. She was still sore from giving birth, but the pain was tempered with a love deeper than she'd ever experienced before.

They'd opened gifts already and taken a break while the last few details of Christmas dinner were taken care of. The smells coming from the kitchen had her drooling. There was no way she was walking away from this meal without chastising herself for eating too much.

Bandit slipped his arm across her shoulders as they sat in the living room of Bear's home. Not only were the entire West and Frederick families there, but her family as well. It was a little tight, and typically she'd feel out of place, except this year was different for so many reasons.

A peace she'd never before had settled in her spirit right after Christopher's birth. She wasn't sure she'd ever be delighted over her weight, but for the first time in her life, she was okay with that. Maybe it wasn't exactly peace. Maybe more like contentment. She had one love of her life sitting next to her, and she was holding the other.

She looked at Bandit. "I think this is the best Christmas I've ever had."

"I think so too." He smiled. "I'm sitting next to the most beautiful woman in the room who is holding the most beautiful baby I've ever seen."

"I love you."

"I love you too." He reached into his shirt pocket and pulled a small card out, handing it to her. "I didn't really want you to open this in front of everyone."

She took the card and looked it over. "What is it?"

"Open it," he said, taking Christopher from her. "I hope you like it."

Keeping her gaze locked with his, she pulled open the envelope flap. She held his gaze one last second and then looked down. She gasped, and her head jerked up. "What?"

It was a property listing for a bed and breakfast located in the Black Hills of South Dakota. A few pictures slipped out, and she looked through them. The place seemed to be hidden from the world with a river that wasn't all that far from the house. The place needed some work, but she could see so much potential.

"We talked about opening our own place. I know you have the flower shop, and if you don't want to do it, you don't have to. I just…"

Skye cupped his cheek. "This is perfect."

"Yeah?"

"Yeah," she said, laughing. "I was going to see what you thought about me selling the shop and finding a place like that."

"Well, we are a pair, huh?"

She kissed him. "I so love you."

"I love you too, sweetheart." He smiled and looked at Christopher and then back to Skye. "I love you both."

For a list of all books by Bree Livingston, please visit her website at www.breelivingston.com.

Bree Livingston lives in the West Texas Panhandle with her husband, children, and cats. She'd have a dog, but they took a vote and the cats won. Not in numbers, but attitude. They wouldn't even debate. They just leveled their little beady eyes at her and that was all it took for her to nix getting a dog. Her hobbies include...nothing because she writes all the time.

She loves carbs, but the love ends there. No, that's not true. The love usually winds up on her hips which is why she loves writing romance. The love in the pages of her books are sweet and clean, and they definitely don't add pounds when you step on the scale. Unless of course, you're actually holding a Kindle while you're weighing. Put the Kindle down and try again. Also, the cookie because that could be the problem too. She knows from experience.

Join her mailing list to be the first to find out publishing news, contests, and more by going to her website at https://www.breelivingston.com.

facebook.com/BreeLivingstonWrites
twitter.com/BreeLivWrites
instagram.com/breelivwrites
bookbub.com/authors/bree-livingston
amazon.com/author/breelivingston